AN UNEXPECTED ADVENTURE

KANDI J. WYATT

United States, 2018

This is a work of fiction. Names, characters, places, brands, media, and incidents are either the product of the author's imagination or are used fictitiously. Any resemblance to similarly named places or to persons living or deceased is unintentional.

:

ACKNOWLEDGMENTS

The making of a book is never done in a vacuum. This book is no exception. From inspiration to final production many have helped make this the best it can be. Thanks to Hunter Jordan, Mason MacFarlane, Chante Combs, and Tyler Mendell for giving me an idea to write this trilogy. Another inspiration for the story is Mr. Betz, my own kids' junior high math and science teacher who challenged students to do their best and loved teaching. Since I knew the kids who I based my characters on, I wanted to try something different for the cover. A fun photoshoot with Eric Wyatt Photography was the result. From that, Amalia Chitulescu worked her magic and created the fantasy feel.

Ally Morcom put her heart and soul into *An Unexpected Adventure*, and it was her suggestion that adjusted the name for both the trilogy and the individual books. My beta readers: Anne Riener, Laura Dickey, Jennifer Lapachian and Cheryll McMahon, did an awesome job and validated several points Ally made later. Sheri Williams has stuck with me through six books now. I couldn't do it without her final touch as proofreader.

Last but not least, thank you, my readers, for sticking with me and encouraging me to continue writing.

*To my junior high Spanish classes in Spring 2015,
and all rural American students.
May you always realize that you are just perfect
the way you are. You've got the best of
America at your fingertips.*

TABLE OF CONTENTS

CHAPTER 1: A FRIDAY NIGHT

"PSST, HARLEY." CHERISE'S voice, although quiet for her, was loud enough to get us into trouble with Miss Smith. "Harley!"

I looked up with an internal sigh, but what else was I supposed to do? Cherise was one of four girls in my eighth-grade class, and my best friend, Chace, had a crush on her. I couldn't make her mad.

"What?" I whispered back, making sure Miss Smith wasn't watching us yet.

Cherise placed both hands on the back of her desk and leaned her pixie face over mine, her big eyes eager.

"Whatcha doin' after school today? Can you come over?"

"I don't know. I've got track practice, and then I have to help Mom and Dad with the B&B."

"Ooh!" Her brown eyes got even bigger, which should have been impossible. She leaned even further onto my desk. "Anyone famous staying there?"

I shook my head. My parents ran, Aidan's Keep, one of the two bed and breakfasts in our little town, and Cherise always expected someone famous to come through. We got our tourists for sure—they came to fish in the ocean or up Myrtle River, windsurf in the lake north of town, or bike the Pacific Coast Trail. Why would anyone famous want to come to little ol' Myrtle Beach, Oregon? Sure, it was rumored that Brad Pitt (or his mom, depending on who you talked with) had a house in the town south of us, but that wasn't Myrtle Beach where the sheep, cattle, and cranberries outnumbered the people.

Cherise's face fell at my answer, then lit up again, and, in a logic all her own, she said, "Then you *can* come over tonight!"

I was saved a comment by Miss Smith.

"Cherise and Harley, stop talking. And Cherise, please sit correctly. In your *own* desk."

"Yes, Miss Smith," we said in unison.

No one messed with Miss Smith, not even Tanner and Peter, the duo that gave every teacher a headache. She used to teach first grade, but due to budget cuts she was moved to the junior high Language Arts class. She still had a no-nonsense way about her that made us all pay attention.

Cherise gave me a wink as she turned around, and I almost laughed out loud at her expression. I rolled my eyes instead and focused back on the class.

*   *   *

You'd think that Cherise would have been satisfied and not bothered me again, but no—not her. Later, on the bus to the high school where we had PE, Spanish, and our elective, I was sitting chatting with my two friends, Will and Chace. We were interrupted by Cherise's head popping up and over the seat in front of Chace and me. Across the aisle, Will laughed. Cherise and Chace glared at him, while I just shook my head.

"What?" Will protested. "You should have seen the two of you jump."

Cherise just tossed her head, her hair bouncing around her chin. "Hey, guys, want to come over tonight? I've got Cabela's Hunt for Wii."

I could tell Chace was tempted. He loved hunting, probably more than any of us.

"I'd need a ride home," he said.

I groaned. Since he lived twelve miles up Myrtle River on a windy, narrow road, that meant I'd have to ask someone from my family to give him a lift. Mom and Dad would be busy with Aidan's Keep B&B, and my older sister, Karis, wasn't a fan of playing chauffeur. "Oh, all right," I said to spare his dignity. "I'll see what I can do."

Cherise's big brown eyes beamed at me. "Thanks, Harley. You won't regret it."

Oh, maybe not because of anything she or my buddies would do, but I'd have to do extra chores tomorrow to make it up to my family. I didn't have time to answer, though, because the bus pulled into the high school, announced by the speed bump and the groans as our classmates were tossed about. Our driver had hit the pot hole right after the speed bump.

"Sure wish someone'd fix that." Chace rubbed his chin where it had bumped against Cherise's seat.

"You know what they say about the school not having money." Will shrugged.

"They're going to have less when they have to replace my tooth," Chace grumbled.

* * *

"Harley Maegher, get in here right now!"

That didn't bode well. When anyone used my last name, I knew I'd done something wrong. When my mom used it, I'd usually left something in the way of guests.

"What is it, Mom?" I asked, all innocence, as I rounded the kitchen door.

I was greeted not by a smiley, happy figure welcoming me home from school, but by one with a frown on her face and hands on her hips.

"How many times do I have to tell you to put your breakfast bowl in the dishwasher before you leave for school?"

"But, Mom—"

"No 'But Mom's.' Professor Raleigh was greeted by a messy breakfast table when he came down today. He's a long-term guest. You can't keep doing that."

"Yes, Mom." I knew the opportune times to argue with her, and this wasn't one of them, especially if I was going to try to get Chace permission to spend the night and go over to Cherise's house, too.

"I'll put the dishes away for you." The open dishwasher had inspired me.

Mom looked at me with a question on her face, but didn't say anything. She was busy getting dinner ready.

About halfway through the job, I asked Mom about our family plans for the evening.

"What's up your sleeve, Harley?" she replied.

I looked up my t-shirt sleeve exaggeratedly. "An arm?"

"Very funny. What do you want to do?"

I told her about Chace wanting to come over and Cherise's invite to play games. She eyed me, a spatula in one hand and her other on the counter.

"What kind of games, Harley?"

"She said she'd gotten the newest Cabela's Hunt."

"You know our rules; nothing over E10+ ratings."

"But, Mom, it's hunting! It's going to have a T rating for the shooting."

Mom nodded, turned, and stirred the meat frying in the skillet. When she was done, she turned back to me.

"I know I can't control your friends in their own homes." She stirred the meat again and then clicked off the stove. "You can play the Cabela's game, but not anything else above E10+. How's Chace getting here?"

I shrugged. "I don't know."

"Uh-huh. I thought so," she said knowingly as she poured sauce over the freshly cooked meat. "You'll have to see if Karis will take you to pick him up."

I nodded. "Thanks, Mom."

*   *   *

We had a great night. The game was fun, but Cherise's parents kicked us out by eight o'clock. It was still light out, so we walked down to the docks where Will spent most of his waking hours when he wasn't in school or hanging out with us. The Crab Shack was closed, though, so we didn't stay for long.

Once the twilight started to deepen, we walked Will home. Sometimes I felt sorry for him. His parents both worked to make ends meet, but it didn't give them any energy left over to parent him. His house had the feel of a morgue—not that I'd ever been in one—and we made a pretty quick exit once we'd seen him safely to the door

When we got back home, we tried to come in quietly, but were met on the porch by Professor Raleigh.

"Hi, Professor," I greeted our wiry guest. "How was your day?"

"Quite fine, Harley; quite fine," he said as he pushed up his glasses. He paused at the door and turned. "You have a friend with you."

I nodded. "Chace, this is Professor Raleigh."

The professor nodded and stuck out his hand.

"Nice to meet you, Chace. I'm Dr. Winston P. Raleigh, Professor of Geology at UC Berkley."

Chace was thoroughly impressed. "Whatcha doin' here in Oregon, Professor?"

"Looking for thundereggs, young man. Looking for thundereggs. Rather magnificent creatures if you ask me."

I looked at Chace and raised an eyebrow. I'd never heard rocks being called creatures before.

"They tell us so much about the area when we cut them open," he clarified. "Say!" His face brightened, lightening his dark eyes and skin. "I could use help searching for them. They're quite rare, but I've been told there are some in the area. Would you boys want to help me look? If you found one, I would pay you for it."

Chace and I looked at each other dumbfounded. We really didn't have anything else planned in the morning other than helping clean the bed and breakfast. If I told Mom I was going with a guest, I could probably get out of chores.

"Sure, I'd be interested."

Chace nodded. "I could look upriver on the ranch. Dad might know of some places to look, too."

"Good. Then I will see you in the morning and we'll talk. I'll have to give you some instructions on what to search for."

CHAPTER 2: A SATURDAY FIND

"COME ON, CHACE," I called. "Hurry up!"

Chace groaned. "Harley, you're not going to find one by rushing around."

We'd been out on the beach for the past hour. I'd roamed ahead of Chace, but Will was even farther up the shore. It was a gorgeous May day on the coast. The surf fell lightly against the rocks, and the wind barely moved Chace's hair, though I knew that'd change by the afternoon.

A shout from Will sent us both running. Chace arrived behind me, out of breath. Track had kept me in shape, but even so, I was slightly winded.

"Whatcha... got?" Chace leaned on his thighs to catch his breath.

"I think I found one." Will smoothed sand away from an oblong area as big as a backpack.

The object blended in with the cream of the sand and rocks. Whatever it was, it didn't look like a rock. It was too smooth.

"That looks like an egg.," Chace bent down to examine it closer.

I nodded. It did.

"But that's why they're called thundereggs." Will didn't even pause as he continued to excavate the item in question.

I shrugged, and Chace shook his head while pushing up his glasses.

"We might as well help him." I bent down and began gently uncovering the stone.

Professor Raleigh had been very particular about the condition in which he wanted his thundereggs delivered. In my opinion they were just large rocks. Sure, they're the state stone, but you really couldn't harm them. The point was to crack them open and find the geode inside. But since the professor was the one paying us for the rock, we followed his orders to dig carefully and not damage the rock.

After a few more minutes of digging, the stone came free. Will wriggled it until we could get a grip underneath and lift it out. I really had my doubts we could pick it up; I was sure it'd weigh close to a hundred pounds or more. However, to my surprise, it came free and up without a hitch, absurdly light for its size.

"Should it be this light?" I squinted at the rock in our hands.

"I don't know." Will shrugged his shoulder.

Chace shifted his grip. "I've never seen a single rock this big before. But it should weigh more than this. I still say it's an egg."

I was beginning to believe him, but there were some good reasons to doubt it, too. "What bird's this big, and how did it get here? We're a long way from the game park."

The game park was the closest thing to a zoo we had. They had wild animals and some pet deer, sheep, donkeys, geese, goats, and peacocks to feed. They even had an emu and an ostrich, but I still couldn't imagine either one having an egg quite this size.

Chace shook his head. "I don't know, but listen." He took a free hand and tapped ever so gently on the surface.

It echoed hollowly. Before anyone could say anything, a second fainter tap came as if in reply.

"What in the *world*?" I exclaimed, jumping and almost dropping the thing.

"It's an egg," Chace said with firm conviction. "I don't know what kind yet, but it's an egg."

"Wh-what do we do with it?" Will looked like he wanted to toss it in the ocean.

"We keep it."

Both Will and Chace looked at me as if I had just turned down a shot at a five-point deer during hunting season. I don't know what I was thinking, but suddenly a fierce desire to protect the creature inside came over me

"We *what*?" At that moment, Will's eyes were as big as Cherise's.

"Where?" Chace was more reasonable. "Your mom won't let you."

"It's not staying at my house!" Will's voice quavered ever so slightly.

We stood holding the strange egg, each of us with a hand on the shell, and when Chace and Will started looking first at me, then at each other, I knew they felt it, too. Wherever our palms rested, there was a pulse of warmth. Chace looked away first, his green eyes focusing on the mystery we held. I couldn't see them behind his glasses, but his face softened. He nodded his head.

"I'll take it." Will and I looked at him with expressions somewhere between relief and uncertainty. "I'll do it. There's the barn that old man Thompson hasn't used in years. No one ever goes in there. There's old hay for a nest, and I can check on it every day."

"Are you sure?" I asked. "I can always try it for a few days."

"Yeah, and what happens if it hatches while we're at school, huh? What then?"

He had me, and he knew it, but I didn't want to give up. Just as I had wanted to protect it, now I found that I didn't want to let it leave my sight.

"What if I keep it for the weekend, bring it to school, and let you take it home?"

Chace eyed me. It was the same calculating look he gave me over a game of soccer. He wondered how serious I was. I began to wonder if he had experienced the same surge of protectiveness for the creature. He nodded.

It was a lot harder to do than to say. The egg was probably a couple of feet long and more than two hands wide. Its surface was smooth as the handlebars on my bike. Only Will's backpack was big enough for it, but he didn't want anything to do with carrying it and made that known in no uncertain terms. In the end, we switched packs. I let him have mine for the weekend.

At home, I took it upstairs to my room where I hid it in a pile of blankets in my closet.

Later that night, Professor Raleigh greeted me on his way to his room. "Any luck today, Harley?"

I shook my head. "No, sir. We didn't find any thundereggs. What about you?"

"Not yet, son. Well, keep looking. I know there's one out there."

*   *   *

My backpack felt awkward as I stepped onto the bus on Monday. I just knew someone was going to notice the odd shape, and we'd lose our egg. All weekend long I'd been nervous. I'd been afraid Mom or Dad would think I was acting strange and get me to confess. They hadn't, but I'd be glad to hand it over to Chace, protective instinct or no.

One look at Will's face, and I knew he hadn't forgiven me for keeping the egg. He hadn't said a word to me at church yesterday, but I'd hoped he'd give in. It didn't look good.

"Hi!" I greeted him as I sat down.

He turned and looked out the window. Great. Kids *might* not look at my backpack, but they most certainly would notice Will was in a tiff. With a sigh I leaned back for the half-hour bus ride.

It was a quiet, awkward trip. Will talked over the seat with Cherise once she got on, but he ignored me. I don't know how Cherise didn't notice, but then again, it was Cherise. No one ever knew what she was thinking.

The students filed off the bus with the typical complaints of junior highers mingling with the enthusiasm of kindergartners. Once in the halls, the elementary kids split off down their corridor and the junior high students went to their lockers.

Chace wasn't anywhere to be seen. I had a dilemma on my hands—the egg barely fit in my locker, and I didn't want to leave it unattended, but the rules said no backpacks in the cafeteria, which was where we spent the first fifteen minutes before the bell rang. I decided to chance it and left the bag in the cramped steel confines, feeling a spike of guilt as I walked away.

Even though Mom had fed me breakfast at home, I decided to grab a bowl of cereal and a carton of milk. If we had to sit in the cafeteria, I might as well eat, and besides, breakfast was free. I grabbed my food and headed to the eighth grade table. To my relief, I spotted Chace finishing his bowl of cereal as I sat down.

"How was your weekend?" I peeled the cover off the cereal packet and opened my milk.

Chace eyed me, but shrugged. "Okay, I guess. Saturday afternoon I helped Dad worm sheep."

"Ew!"

Chace grinned. "It's better than docking tails."

"True," I agreed. "But I'd rather be beach combing."

Chace pushed up his glasses. "How was yours?"

I twitched a shoulder. "Okay. Nothing exciting."

Chace nodded. "Do you have your backpack back?"

I shook my head. "Probably after school."

"Any problem using the other one?"

I knew what he meant. He was asking about the egg. I shook my head. My mouth was full of cereal. He rolled his eyes and dropped his elbows onto the table. I swallowed and looked around. Everyone else was at the other end of the table chatting.

"It's fine. I have it in my locker," I said in a conspiratorial tone.

Even behind his glasses I could see the surprise register in his eyes.

"I wasn't going to break school rules to bring it in here." I glanced around nervously.

Chace relaxed. "Bring it to class."

"Of course."

I knew it was risky, but I'd just have to take that chance. I couldn't leave it alone all day.

When the bell rang, I grabbed my garbage, tossed it in the trash, and got in line. I found myself next to Chace at the end.

"What's up with Will?" He nodded toward our friend.

"He's still mad. He'll come around."

It wasn't what Chace wanted to hear; he disliked conflict more than the average person. Usually we all got along, but sometimes

Will could be, well, Will, and Will had a mind of his own. Chace and I both knew to give him a few days, and he'd likely come around.

*   *   *

Between second and third period we had our break. I took my backpack toward the restroom.

"Harley," Miss Smith called from her doorway. "You know better than to take your bag into the restroom, or to class for that matter. What's so important that you can't leave it in your locker?"

"Ah, nothing, ma'am."

She gave me her famous stare, the one that made first grade students cry and hardened junior high boys shake in their boots.

"We found a rock on the beach on Saturday," I said, scrambling for a plausible excuse. I was surprised and a little impressed with my own ingenuity when the next words that came out were: "We wanted to show it to Mr. Behr to see what kind it is."

She nodded. "It must be pretty big. Go ahead and take it to him then."

"Yes, Miss Smith."

My heart sank. What had I *done*? But there was no backing out now. Miss Smith was watching me like a hawk. I had to go to Mr. Behr's room now, so I crossed my fingers and hoped he just wasn't there.

"Hi, Harley; hi Chace," Mr. Behr's deep and kind voice greeted me. I was surprised to turn and see that Chace was, indeed, behind me. "What can I do for you boys?"

I looked to Chace, but he hid behind his glasses and bangs. There was no help there.

"We were wondering if you knew what this was." I said setting the backpack on one of the lab tables.

Mr. Behr taught both math and science, and he was one of my favorite teachers. He genuinely liked the students, and it showed. Right now, he stood waiting with his hands resting on his ample stomach. Give him white hair, and with his round belly and beard he'd look just like Santa Claus.

Chace cleared his throat, and I swallowed. After a furtive look, I unzipped the backpack and carefully began to reveal the egg. Chace reached out a hand and caressed it. The gesture surprised me. Our eyes locked. An understanding passed between us, a pledge in the midst of a tense and uncertain moment.

"That's some find," Mr. Behr said. "Where'd you get it?"

I told him about Professor Raleigh and how he was looking for thundereggs.

Leaning in closer for a look, Mr. Behr asked, "May I?"

At a nod from both of us, he reached out and touched the shell. After a brief moment of contact, his bushy eyebrows suddenly leapt up as if trying to jump off his face. Without a word, he walked to the door and shut it. Returning, he placed both hands on the egg.

"Boys, what do you know about thundereggs?"

Both Chace and I shrugged, intrigued by Mr. Behr's behavior. "They're large rocks?" Chace finally voiced his thoughts.

Mr. Behr nodded, waiting.

"Sometimes, they can have quartz inside of them," I said. "And they're the state rock."

Mr. Behr nodded again. "You *have* been paying attention in class. Now, I'm going to ask you to apply what you know. Where are thundereggs found?"

I looked to Chace. He didn't remember. I paused, trying to think back to sixth grade science class. It seemed so long ago.

"I knew it!" The words seemed to explode from Chace. "Something didn't seem right, Harley, when the professor said he was looking for thundereggs. We have agates on the beach, not thundereggs. Those are found in the center of the state!"

Mr. Behr shifted to readjust his weight. We looked to him.

"Boys, feel the outside of this."

Chace and I caressed the egg. It was silky smooth.

"Thundereggs are rough until polished. This shows no signs of polishing. It's way too big to be an agate. How heavy is it?"

I shrugged. "I don't want to carry it around all day, but it's not bad in the backpack."

"It's mainly bulky," Chace's words had shifted to what they were like during science class, all business and thoughtful. Mr. Behr had trained us to talk like scientists. I picked up on the cue.

"Then why would Professor Raleigh say he knows there's thundereggs here? He's a professor at UC Berkley."

"Remember, Harley, even teachers and professors can be wrong. We're all learning," Mr. Behr reminded us.

The bell rang, causing us all to jump.

"Would you trust me to keep it here?" Mr. Behr asked.

I looked to Chace.

"I'm taking it home tonight," he said.

"What if I drop it off at the high school for you before you get on the bus?"

Chace's eyes got large. "You're *serious*?"

"Come in at lunch and we'll talk about it."

CHAPTER 3: A LUNCHTIME MEETING

WHEN THERE ARE only eighteen people in your whole class, they notice when one of your best friends doesn't hang out with you. By lunch, everyone was talking about Will not talking to me. I was glad the egg was with Mr. Behr—I was afraid Will would say something out of spite. I should have known better, but sometimes Will could get snippy, and I never knew what he'd do.

"Hey, Harley," Tanner called from a table where he sat. "Come eat over here. I can be your new friend."

Peter and the other boys at the table laughed. I ignored them and waited for Chace to grab his lunch. Once he was through the line, we headed for the door.

"Boys." Claudia, the lunch lady, stopped us at the door. "You know you can't take food out of the cafeteria."

"Mr. Behr wants us to see him." Chace juggled his lunch tray to push up his glasses.

Claudia steadied his tray.

"Thanks," he mumbled.

"Go eat then," she said. "But make sure this tray comes back here."

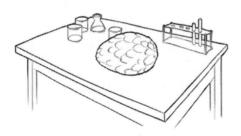

"Yes, ma'am." We agreed and hurried past her.

Once we were settled in the science room with the egg on the lab table, Mr. Behr asked, "What do you boys think this is?"

Chace spoke up before I could. "When Will found it, he thought it was a stone, but I knew it was an egg."

I stared at my best friend, dumbfounded. I thought we were going to protect the egg, and here he was telling a teacher what we thought it was. I kicked him under the table. He glared at me, but continued talking.

"What I don't know is what kind of animal would lay an egg this *huge*."

"Good question, Chace." Mr. Behr nodded. "What about you, Harley? Do you agree with Chace?"

I looked at the egg, trying to decide what to do. We all liked Mr. Behr, but could I trust him? He waited for my answer in his relaxed manner, as if he had all the time in the world. Chace didn't push, waiting for me to make my own decision.

"I guess there's no point denying it now," I sighed. "Yeah, I agree with Chace."

Mr. Behr shifted his position. "Based on what you know, what animal could it be?"

That question had been floating around my head all weekend.

"I've been thinking about that." Chace set his fork down. "The only animals I know of that can be that big are emus, ostriches, and tortoises. Tortoises probably have a smaller egg because they get bigger as they get older. Emus and ostriches aren't this big."

"So, what is it?" I opened my milk and took a drink.

Chace shrugged. "The only thing that makes any sense is something that no longer exists."

I wanted to look at him as if he'd grown horns, but the same thought had come to me. I hoped Mr. Behr would set us straight.

"And what would that be, Chace?"

I couldn't believe our science teacher was encouraging this line of reasoning.

"Dinosaur eggs would be this big." Chace shoved his last bite of food into his mouth.

"A dino?" I asked, trying to sound like I hadn't pondered the idea as well. "How could it be?"

"I don't know." Chace stood and dropped his trash into the garbage can.

I finished my sandwich, hopped down from my chair, and walked over to the egg. Seemingly of its own accord, my hand began caressing its smooth surface. Chace and Mr. Behr joined me.

"Boys, you've done an amazing job of setting out a hypothesis. Now it's time to prove it. I could have a friend at the university test it for age and scan it for clues."

My mind shrank away from the suggestion. I didn't want to hurt the egg that way. Before I could answer, Chace shook his head.

"I don't think so. Thanks for the offer, but. . ." he trailed off.

Mr. Behr nodded. "I understand. Really the process couldn't hurt the egg."

Unless it's alive. The words floated through my mind unbidden. Chace laid his hand on the egg as he thought. Mr. Behr added his. We stood looking at it, trying to puzzle out the mystery. What could it be?

While we pondered, a quiet, pulsing sound filtered into my conscious hearing. It started low, but built in intensity, until I recognized the pattern. It sounded like a heartbeat. Chace stirred beside me, but Mr. Behr held a finger to his lips and shook his head. The beating continued, calm and steady. Mr. Behr was the first to move. I had never seen his face so amazed, peaceful, and curious all at the same time.

"Chace," his voice cracked like a teenager's. "I think I understand your hesitation. Are you still sure you want to take it home tonight?"

Chace nodded. "I can't leave it here."

"Okay." Mr. Behr's voice was back to its normal bass timbre. "Just promise me you'll let me know if you need any help"

We both nodded.

CHAPTER 4: A MYSTERIOUS EGG

THE NEXT MORNING as I ate breakfast, Professor Raleigh came into the dining room. I greeted him but made sure to take another bite so I didn't have to talk to him; unfortunately, it didn't work.

"Harley, why didn't you tell me you boys found a thunderegg this weekend?"

I almost upset my breakfast bowl in shock. "What do you mean?"

"I said I'd pay you for the rock if you found one, but you didn't tell me."

"We didn't find a thunderegg." My mind raced to catch up and hopefully get a step ahead before I let something slip.

"Now, don't lie to me Harley. I know you and your friends found one on Saturday."

"But, honestly, Professor—"

He held up a finger. "Someone who was with you told me all about it. So, before you dig yourself into a hole, why don't you answer my question?"

"Professor, I don't know who you talked to, but Chace and I did *not* find a thunderegg." I gathered the remains of my breakfast. "If I don't take care of this, I'll miss the bus."

I loaded my dishes into the dishwasher, grabbed my backpack, and headed out the door. When the bus came, I greeted the driver and then headed back to where Will sat. He didn't give me any room to join him, but I wasn't going to let that stop me. I pushed him over and thumped my bag down at my feet. He glared at me, then looked down. I must have looked as intimidating as a bull elk whose harem had been threatened.

"Why'd you tell Professor Raleigh that we'd found a thunderegg?" My voice was just loud enough to be heard over the bus engine, but my frustration was completely evident. "What were you *thinking*?"

"I found a thunderegg and you and Chace took it from me." Will's back stayed straight as a board despite the jolting of the bus.

"It's not a thunderegg!" I exclaimed. "Think about it. Have you ever heard of one to be so smooth on the outside? Besides, you felt that tap; a thunderegg doesn't tap back."

"You guys aren't going to cheat me out of that money, Harley. If you don't want it, I'll take it. You know how much we need it."

I flopped back, surprised and a little chastened. I knew money was tight for his family, but I didn't think it was *that* bad!

"Will," I said, softer now, "what if I told you Mr. Behr agrees with us?"

Will's head whipped around to look at me. "Mr. Behr?"

I nodded.

"What about Mr. Behr?" Cherise's voice startled me.

I turned toward the aisle to see her pixie face resting on her hands with her elbows on her knees. Her big brown eyes looked inquisitively at us.

"He doesn't think the rock we found this weekend is a thunderegg." Will glared at me, daring me to contradict him.

Great. Another unknown quantity in on the secret. Knowing Cherise's propensity for chatting, I figured it'd be better if she heard it from Mr. Behr; maybe he could convince her of the seriousness. "Why don't you two talk to him at break?" I suggested, giving in to the inevitable. "Chace and I'll come with you."

*   *   *

Never had the first two periods dragged by so slowly. I don't think Will heard a single word in Language Arts or Social Studies. Every time I looked at him, he was gazing out the windows. All I could think about was the beating of the heart we had heard and felt yesterday at lunch.

As soon as the bell rang, we bolted from our seats. I was glad Miss Smith didn't stop us. We found Mr. Behr in his classroom.

"What brings you all to my room on this fine spring day?" Mr. Behr relaxed with his hands folded on his belly.

Chace shut the door and nodded to me.

"Mr. Behr, Will was the one who found the egg, but he's convinced it's a thunderegg. Can you tell him why it isn't? Oh, and Cherise wants to know, too."

Cherise smiled at me and turned to our math and science teacher. "What he's trying to say is that I'm nosey, and I want to know what the boys are up to."

Mr. Behr's deep, hearty laugh filled the room. "Well what they found is a very rare object. At first they thought it *was* a thunderegg."

He went on to outline how we had ruled out the possibility. When he finished, Will looked up at Mr. Behr.

"What you're saying is that what I found is a dinosaur egg? And not only that, but it's *living*?"

Mr. Behr nodded.

"I think you're all missing something," Cherise surprised us by saying. "Why does it have to be a dinosaur egg? Why not a griffon, or a dragon, or a phoenix?"

I stared at her, dumbstruck. "Really?"

"Is it any more crazy than a living dinosaur?" She lowered her big innocent eyes into a direct challenge, looking at me unblinking.

"I. . ." I closed my mouth.

"Okay, if we assume that our legends of dragons are from dinosaurs, you may be right, Cherise, but I doubt it could be any of the other mythical creatures," Mr. Behr said. "Chace, be careful, and let me know as soon as it hatches."

"Yes, Mr. Behr." Chace stood taller. "I will."

The bell interrupted our conversation. With dragging feet, we headed to our lockers.

"Now I *have* to see this egg," Cherise said.

Chace and I nodded in agreement.

CHAPTER 5: AN EGG HATCHES

DESPITE OUR PROMISE and best intentions, it didn't happen. Life did as it tends to do—run together from one busy task to the next. Track season finished out. We won districts, and I beat my personal record. It was awesome. The others were busy with miscellaneous things. Chace had the farm. The dry spring led to an early summer, so his days were filled with duties that normally happened after school got out. The crab shack kept Will busy. Cherise bugged us to no end, but none of our schedules coincided.

We had only three weeks left of school when I was able to convince Karis to drive Will, Cherise, and me up to Chace's place to swim. Normally, Myrtle River is too cold to swim until July or August, but with the unseasonably warm weather we had had, we figured the river would be fine. Karis dropped us off with instructions to be ready when she came to pick us up.

The water was perfect for swimming, but our attention was elsewhere, and it wasn't long before we'd all dried off and started meandering toward the barn. We stood in the hayloft. Dust motes floated in streams of sunlight where it filtered through old nail holes. I wondered how the roof held up in the winter rains. For now it was perfect—warm, dimly lit, and quiet.

Chace bent down and began to clear the hay away from one area. I could tell he'd done it before, because his movements were tender and practiced. As he piled the hay off to one side, the sandy shell came into view, and we moved in closer, seating ourselves around it. Cherise leaned in with a soft sound of awe, reaching out to touch it, moving as if she were petting one of her dogs. Her motion disrupted my momentary paralysis, and I stretched out a hand to rest on the egg. Chace, too, lay a hand on the shell. That left a spot open for Will. Without a word, all three of us looked to him. He nodded. His hand reached out slowly, as if he was afraid of being burned. The moment all four of us made contact, we heard a faint knocking sound.

I shared a double take with Chace. He gave me a minute shake of his head in answer to my unspoken question. The knocking grew louder until we heard a shattering noise, almost like glass breaking. Startled, we all jumped.

Looking down at the egg, I saw a thin line, almost like purple ink, spreading across the yellow shell. A gasp escaped my mouth, but I didn't have time to say anything. The crack exploded before my eyes, and an amethyst-colored claw poked its way out. We all sat mesmerized as a thin, jointed appendage revealed itself. Another loud retort reverberated through the shell and into our hands. The limbs twitched, showing a thin membrane of the same purple shades. I thought I had seen Cherise's eyes as wide as they could go, but a glance up proved me wrong.

"This is no dinosaur," she said in a quiet voice, so as not to startle the creature hatching beneath our hands.

As if to prove her point, the joints extended and the membrane suddenly stretched wide, revealing their true nature—a wing. Another claw followed, a rending crack appearing right in front of Chace's hand. With his typical nonchalance, he repositioned it so the next wing would have room to escape its prison, which it did a few moments later. There was a pause, probably as the creature rested from its exertion, its two wings still partially spread. Cherise continued caressing what was left of the shell. I stole a glance at Will. His eyes were wide with wonder. Gone was the fear from before. He gently rubbed the piece of shell left in his fingers.

A few moments later, the wings gathered together, and then thrust forward and unfurled to their full span. At the same moment, the loudest crack yet resounded through the hayloft. Will scooted back as a long, barbed tail broke free. Chace held his ground when a horned, serpentine head rose up to meet him. The eyes were like amethyst crystals I'd seen in a gem store, and one was looking directly at me. I couldn't move, transfixed, gazing into its depths.

A sound of air escaping from Will broke the spell. The eye and the rest of the head turned away from me and toward Chace and Will. I looked from one to the other as the little baby took us all in.

Never had I seen anything like it—not even when I saw Will's rabbit give birth. A feeling of peace, loyalty, and safety began in the corners of my heart and seeped out into every fiber of my body. Looking round, I saw the same feelings on the faces of my friends, clear as the evening sun reflecting from the ocean.

A miniature explosion from the dragon (there was no denying the fact) caused the remaining pieces of shell to fall to the hay. The dragon stretched first her neck, then one foot, and then the other, much like a cat waking up from a nap, working out the kinks. With a feeble flapping motion of her wings, she arched her back and pushed off. I held my breath. Her body didn't leave the ground, but a dust storm billowed out around her, and shortly after, a flurry of sneezes and coughs.

How I knew this violet hatchling was a girl was beyond my comprehension. I just knew it, as clearly as I knew my name was Harley Meagher, in the same way I knew I had to protect her and that she wouldn't hurt us.

Having failed at flying, the little creature began to move her feet, which I was surprised to see were dainty and evenly proportioned for her size. We regarded her in silence as she began exploring, snuffling around the loft and occasionally floundering in the deep hay that had been her nest.

Cherise was the first to speak. "I told you it didn't have to be a dinosaur." Her brown eyes never left the small wonder before us.

"We should've believed you," I admitted in a hushed tone.

"What now?" Will shook his head. "What do we do with a dragon?"

Chace followed the creature with his eyes while his hand ran through his hair. I could tell his mind was working as hard as if Mr. Behr had given him an Algebra II problem.

When the dragon turned back toward Chace, she paused and looked him straight in the eyes. It was almost like she was trying to say something. After a few seconds, she resumed her search of the hayloft.

"She'll stay here for now." Chace surprised me.

Will seemed shocked. His voice cracked as he exclaimed, "What? How can you do that?"

"I'll make a guard for the ladder area, and I'll make sure I feed her and check in on her before and after school."

"What will you feed her?" Will asked. Whatever had clued me in about her gender, apparently we had all noticed it.

Chace considered. "For now, I can use some chicken grain. Later, I'll figure out what she needs."

"What are we going to call her?" I tore my gaze off the little dragon to look at my friends.

"Her name, of course!" Cherise stated in her matter of fact way.

"Which is?" Will looked over at the dragon scratching and sniffing in the hay.

That was a good question, and I didn't have an answer. Obviously, Cherise and Chace did, though, for they responded in unison, "Steria!"

The moment the word hit the air, the dragon paused in mid-stride and turned to look at us.

"Steria?" I half called, half asked.

She nodded her head and came toward me. "Hi, girl. I wish you could tell us how you came to be on the shoreline."

I do not know, a soft, melodic female voice resonated in my head. *Only darkness until. . .* she trailed off and looked around.

Sunlight filtered through the dust Steria had stirred up, and a fly buzzed in the corner. We stared at her, dumbfounded. Will scooted even farther away.

What? she thought at us, glancing at each of our faces.

"Um… you can talk," I stammered dumbly.

You do.

"Yeah, but…"

Chace cut me off and said, "You said you only knew darkness until… until what?"

Until you came and woke me. The light poured in, and I had to move and meet you face to face.

I stared at her amazed. We had awakened her? But how?

Will? she asked.

He peered at her quizzically.

Ah, you first disturbed my sleep. Then you, Harley. She turned to look at me, her eyes almost glowing with an inner light. *You believed from the first. I had to wake up.*

I stared amazed at her words. I had encouraged her to awaken? She turned again. This time I saw tenderness come into her eyes, almost like a puppy looking at its owner.

Chace. She stepped forward to his outstretched hand. A pang of jealously flickered through me. *Do not worry, Harley,* whispered in my ears, and I knew instinctively that no one else had heard Steria's words to me.

She laid her scaly head into Chace's palm. *Thank you for protecting me.*

"Aw, it was nothing," Chace replied, but a shy smile flickered across his lips.

She lifted her head, flicked her tail, and flapped her wings. With fluttering hops, she moved to Cherise.

From the first, you knew who I was. Maybe because we are both female, we share a different bond.

She paused and looked around as if searching for something or someone. *But there was one more.* Her voice was confused. *Where is he?*

My eyes met Chace's. He shrugged just as puzzled as I was.

"Who, Steria?" Cherise asked.

A man, jolly and kind.

"Mr. Behr!" Will's face lit up with understanding.

I nodded. "That was our science teacher, Steria. He's at his home."

A sadness touched the emotions coming from the little dragon. She seemed to process the thought, and then moved away from

Chace. A fly darted in front of her. Quicker than I thought possible, she snaked her neck forward, and chomped, but came down on thin air. With a shake of her head, she ran after the fly. I smiled. It was so much like a kitten.

Cherise laughed out loud. "That's like Finn chasing the laser light," she said, referring to her black lab.

"Harley!" Karis' voice drifted on the breeze blowing between the chinks in the boards.

"Quick!" Panic seized me. "Will come with me. Chace, get Steria and keep her safe."

I didn't look to see if anyone else moved. I had to keep my sister out of here. She couldn't see Steria. I took the ladder, but my feet barely touched the wooden rungs, and I felt the slivers pile up as my hands slid down the sides. I reached the bottom and headed for the door in my best track run. Reaching the empty doorway, I about ran into Karis.

"Harley Meagher, where are you?" she called, her voice echoing in my ears.

"I'm right here."

She jumped with shock. "Where'd you come from?" Her hands, having first gone above her head in fright, now settled down on her hips like a buzzard landing.

"We were helping Chace with a chore," I said, surprised I could think straight enough to not lie to her, but still not say what we were really doing.

She looked at Will, who nodded agreement. I held my breath. Would she accept it? Slowly, her stance changed.

"Where's Cherise? It's time to head home."

"I'm right here," Cherise's voice made me jump; I hadn't heard her come up behind us.

Karis shook her head and eyed me suspiciously, but thankfully, she seemed to think little enough of it that she turned back toward the car

"Come on, then. Let's go."

The ride back home was quiet. I occupied myself plucking the slivers out of my hands, which was no easy task in the bouncing car. The wood had sunk deep into the flesh. I counted twenty thin slips of wood that I pulled out of my palms and fingers by the time we made it back to town.

Karis dropped Will and Cherise off at their homes. As the car pulled into the drive, she turned to me.

"Harley, I don't know what you're up to, but if I find out you've lied to me, I'll tell Mom and Dad."

"I didn't." I was glad I could answer her truthfully.

"You weren't doing any ordinary chore. Your friends were too guilty looking."

"It was a project," I amended my earlier statement.

I saw the question coming in the lift of her eyebrow and stalled it by saying, "It's a science project for Mr. Behr."

She smiled and nodded. "Is this anything to do with your eighth-grade project? Why didn't you say so?"

She climbed out, leaving me speechless. Why hadn't I thought of that? Steria could fit in biology. For once my sister had helped me out, even though she hadn't planned on it.

CHAPTER 6: A SCIENCE PROJECT

"YOU HAVE A *what*?" Mr. Behr's face was as red as I had ever seen it.

None of us had expected that reaction. All four of us had gathered in his classroom first thing Monday morning, eager to tell him about Steria. It was Cherise who seemed to calm him down.

"Mr. Behr." Her dark eyes shone in a way I had never seen before. "You should have seen it. The egg cracked and her eyes were like your amethyst geodes you've shown us. But she knew you weren't there. She asked about you."

He stood back, his arms crossed and resting on his belly. I could see his mind spinning.

"She asked about me?"

"Yep!" Cherise nodded. "She wondered where you were."

"Okay, I guess I'll have to meet her before I make any judgment calls. My instinct says all of this is crazy, but... I heard her just as clearly as you all have seen her. I thought I was just hearing things."

"You could come over after school," Chace offered.

As if finally giving in, Mr. Behr nodded his head. "Okay. Do any of the rest of you want to come along?"

Of course we all did. School couldn't let out fast enough.

* * *

Mr. Behr made us all call our parents to get permission to ride with him out to Chace's place. Chace rode the bus home, but Cherise, Will and I crowded into the blue Ford F150 double cab and buckled up. Energy buzzed through us as if we were hyped up on candy.

Finally, the pickup pulled to a stop beside the barn, and we all piled out. Chace met us.

"Dad's not home yet, but Steria's up and eager to see everyone."

He led us up the loft ladder where the sunlight no longer reached. Our eyes had to adjust. When they did, the hay was all we saw. I was puzzled. Where was the little dragon? Mr. Behr sucked in air and then gave a thready whistle.

"She's beautiful!"

I followed his gaze and found her, standing on a railing with her wings outspread as if to keep her balance. Her gem-like eyes regarded Mr. Behr.

Welcome, her gentle voice echoed in my mind. *Thank you for coming, Mr. Behr.*

"I had to see for myself."

Am I real? the dragon asked teasingly, jumping down into the hay and making her way toward us.

Mr. Behr shook his head. "My eyes say yes, but my mind still says it's impossible." He bent down, and Steria rubbed up against his leg. He laughed that deep, sonorous laugh. "You feel hard as a gemstone."

All dragons have hard scales, Steria stated.

Mr. Behr stood up. "Chace, what are you feeding her?"

"Fish and grain for the chickens."

Mr. Behr nodded. "Then for now she's okay up here. When she gets bigger we'll have to figure out different arrangements."

After another fifteen minutes of disbelieving queries and exclamations, Mr. Behr threw up his hands. "I'll never manage to ask everything I want to in a single afternoon. Why don't we come by after school each day? We can check in on Steria, and I can satisfy my scientific curiosity."

*   *   *

Thus began our very late eighth grade biology project. Mr. Behr made sure we were taking field notes on what Steria ate, how much she grew, and her abilities. Chace's dad was rarely at home. With the unseasonable heat, logging had been shut down except for early mornings, so his afternoons were spent on the fishing boats. Cherise's folks didn't seem to mind the extra hours she was spending with the boys, but I wasn't sure if she phrased it that way or if she said that she was working on a school project. I'm not even sure if Will's parents even knew his schedule was any different. My sister was the most curious of all the 'adults' in my life.

"Harley," she said one night around the dinner table, "You never said what you're studying for your science project."

I was thankful for the hours with Mr. Behr, as we'd worked out a truthful answer to give her.

"It's a lizard we found."

"What kind?"

I did some quick thinking and didn't miss a beat. "A dragon lizard."

"No way!" Karis said. "I bet it was one that was a pet and got away."

I let her think what she would. "Since it's a special kind of lizard, Mr. Behr is helping us and letting us all work on the project."

"Well, you'd better do a good job. When I had to do my project, we didn't get Mr. Behr's personal help. He made us work for it."

I nodded and hurried away from the table, mumbling about homework.

*   *   *

When we showed up the next night, Steria wasn't in the hayloft. If it wasn't for Mr. Behr, we would have panicked. He made us look around and then call to her. We searched the whole barn.

"Steria!" we all shouted at various levels of stress. "Steria, where are you?"

I didn't hear anything, but it was almost as if something told me to be still. I stopped. That same nagging thought told me to listen. I was surprised to feel—not hear—laughter. It was coming from. . . I turned around and looked up. There, tucked into the cross braces of the roof, sat the purple dragon.

Shh, she said into my mind. There was a chuckle blended with her warning.

I shook my head. How had she gotten up there? Confounded, I watched as she swung down and glided to the floor at my feet, her movements much like those of a bat. Then she rubbed her head against my leg. I stood stunned for a moment, then dropped to my knees and petted her hard, scaly body.

"Where was she?" Chace's voice startled me.

I pointed. He nodded and wiped his hair out of his eyes. "She's been going higher in the hayloft, but I didn't think she'd come down here."

"She flew." I marveled.

"She's a dragon," Cherise said, coming up beside me.

"That's what they do." Will wiped his hands on his shorts.

Mr. Behr just stared.

Steria sat basking in the attention. Without any warning, she bounded off; with a leap she was in the air and there was a fly trapped in her jaws. Her path swerved and another flying insect met its demise.

"Well," Mr. Behr broke the stunned silence. "Our baby is now a toddler. We're going to have our hands full."

CHAPTER 7: A SECRET DISCOVERED

SCHOOL WAS WINDING down, with our eighth grade recognition and field trip the day after only a week away. As we passed Seashore B&B on our way to school, I saw Professor Raleigh. The professor was packing a machine into the trunk of a white Ford Taurus, a vehicle that stood out like a bear in San Francisco. It was too clean for one, and it wasn't a pickup or a minivan. I didn't see the license plate, but the vehicle itself would be easy to spot.

I rode the bus with Chace to his ranch after school. As we entered the barn our eyes had to adjust to the dim light. I looked around, but couldn't see Steria. I had yet to glimpse her. I decided to head up to the loft to see if she was there, but all her usual perches among the rafters were empty. I spun around, dazed.

"Chace, where is she?" I heard the fear in my own voice.

"Call her," Chace answered. "I suggest you go back down first, though."

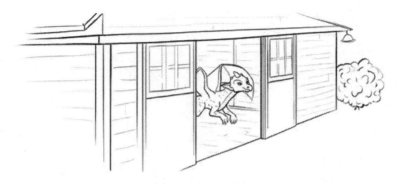

We had worked with Steria to come when we called. We usually called out loud, but lately she wanted us just to be quiet and think her name. Chace's laughter seemed to be bubbling up inside of him. Suddenly, I realized it wasn't him laughing, but Steria.

Where are *you?* Frustration tinged my thought.

Harley. Steria's voice echoed through my mind. *I'm coming.*

"Coming?"

We'd reached the main floor when a rushing of wind filled our ears. I looked to the door just in time to see a purple streak flying toward me.

"She just started that this morning." Chace grinned at my shocked look.

We spent the rest of the afternoon working with Steria as she flew in and out of the barn, around the pasture and to the forest beyond. Karis showed up to pick me up while Steria was in the trees.

"I'll see you tomorrow, at school." I waved to Chace and headed toward the car.

However, right at that moment, Steria decided to return to the barn. Her flight pattern led her directly in front of my sister. Karis screamed, threw up her hands to protect her face, and dove to the ground. Steria landed at my feet and beside Karis on the floor.

Why is she down here? Steria's voice no longer was one of a little girl, but the dulcet tone of a cultured lady.

"Steria!" I scolded out loud, surprised that she'd even show herself to someone besides our small group.

Karis straightened up and brushed the dirt from her jeans. When she paused, her green eyes grew large.

"A dragon lizard?"

Steria sat on her haunches, her wings folded against her back, her head now level with my waist. She stretched her neck toward me, her scales glittering in the light streaming in through the doorway.

"Not a lizard," Karis continued. "A real, live dragon...!" Awe filled her voice.

Your sister? Steria looked up at me.

I nodded. "Karis, meet Steria. Steria, meet Karis."

Hello, Steria replied. *Why did you scream?*

"You scared me!" Karis said. "It's not everyday a creature as big as the barn door flies at me."

Steria just blinked at her. *I would not have hurt you.*

She turned and leaped. The motion no longer bore any resemblance to her first awkward jump from her shell; it was a graceful push and glide away from the ground. As soon as she cleared the floor, her wings spread out to their full span. With one mighty push she lifted higher into the air. Clearing the door, she beat her wings again and emitted a screech unlike anything I had ever heard before. With steady flapping, she soared into the air, after which she must have caught an air current, and we watched her glide, graceful as a hawk. I could feel her contentment, and a little sparkling mote of pride that she hoped I wouldn't notice. I laughed and thought, *Look at you!*

Her satisfaction redoubled as she circled the weather vane atop the roof.

Karis stood with her mouth hanging open. She didn't close it until Steria had landed back at our feet.

"Tell me the *whole* story," Karis demanded.

So we did. Together, Chace and I told her everything.

* * *

Three miles down the road at Cabbage Creek Campground a white Ford Taurus sat alongside the road. It was deserted. My stomach turned as I remembered seeing Professor Raleigh packing his car. Could this be his? If so, was he searching for Steria? Unfortunately, at the time there was nothing I could do about it other than mention to Karis what I knew. When we arrived home, I called Chace to warn him that the professor could be prowling around near the ranch. Unfortunately, he didn't answer. I went to bed with an unsettled feeling in the pit of my stomach.

CHAPTER 8: A HAIR-RAISING EXPERIENCE

THE NEXT DAY, I was finally able to make contact with Chace and relay my concerns.

"Harley, I'll keep my eyes out, but I don't know what else I can do at the moment."

Unfortunately, I realized he was right. I wished I could chat with Mr. Behr, but what kid called a teacher on the weekend?

Sunday after church I hung out with Will at the crab shack, and nothing major happened. I counted down the hours until we'd go to school. How lame is that? Lacking anything constructive to do with my worry, I tried to write it off as paranoia, and partly succeeded. Sort of. It still stuck like a burr in the back of my mind, but I managed to at least tell myself that everything would be fine and pretend to believe it.

Monday dawned bright and beautiful. We had only three days of school left. Nothing could dampen my enthusiasm. That is, until the bus passed Seashore B&B and I saw Professor Raleigh packing his machine into that Ford Taurus.

At school, I didn't wait for Chace or any of the others. I went directly to Mr. Behr's room and spilled my worries like pebbles on the beach.

Mr. Behr listened. "Harley, until the professor crosses onto private property, there's nothing we can do."

"That's just it!" I exclaimed. "There's no one home at Chace's. His dad's off logging, and he's here. Anyone could go there right now, and no one would know."

"There is that, but from what we've seen, Steria's big enough to take care of herself."

I shook my head. I didn't like it, but if the only adult in the know wasn't going to do anything, there wasn't anything left for me to try. With a sigh, I left to grab my books for class.

The day dragged on. Nothing cheered me up. At last, the final bell rang, and I grabbed my backpack to leave. Will and Cherise were going straight home. They couldn't convince their folks to let them hang out at Chace's now that our eighth grade projects were finished, but Karis had spoken up for me to Mom and Dad. So it was just Mr. Behr and me as we went up Myrtle River Road that afternoon. We enjoyed a companionable silence until we rounded Cabbage Creek. Along the side of the road was the white Taurus.

"Mr. Behr!" I shouted, "That's the professor's car."

We slowed, but didn't stop. From there on out, I kept my eyes peeled for Professor Raleigh, scouting the edges of the road and the bank of the river, but I had no luck in the three miles to Chace's driveway. We pulled in and drove down to the barn. The place seemed deserted.

We walked in, but no one was around. I remembered how Steria had communicated with me the week before. I stood still listening for our not-so-little-anymore dragon. I heard nothing. I thought her name and remembered her flying through the barn door. Still nothing.

I looked to Mr. Behr for an answer. He shook his head. We headed out toward Chace's house and down toward the river. All the while I called her name in my mind. Once at the river, I caught a flicker of recognition, and I stopped in my tracks. Mr. Behr continued on, but I ducked behind a tree. I couldn't explain why any more than I could have explained why I wanted to protect Steria before I knew her.

Peering around the tree trunk, I saw Mr. Behr stroll down the rock-strewn river bank and up to a man bent over. No one should have been here other than Chace and his dad. When the man straightened up at Mr. Behr's greeting, I sucked in my breath. It was Professor Raleigh! At his feet, his machine was emitting a rhythmic clicking sound. Mr. Behr chatted for a while and pointed to the box on the river rock. The professor gestured and spoke in response, but I was too far away to make out what he had said. I wanted to know what they were saying, but knew I needed to stay hidden. Before too long, Mr. Behr shook Professor Raleigh's hand, waved, and came back toward me. He walked on past me, then turned into the trees and backtracked to where I was.

"How did you know to hide, Harley?" he asked peering around the tree out toward the river.

"I don't know. It was almost like Steria told me to."

"That's interesting." Mr. Behr turned back to me. "She told *me* to go down by the river. She'll meet us back at the barn."

"Is it safe? Won't Professor Raleigh follow us?"

"I don't think so. I warned him about private property in this area, and explained that even the river bank could get him in trouble if a farmer wanted to press the issue."

"Did he ask why you were here?"

Mr. Behr shook his head. "No, but I told him I was here on scientific business and had the owner's permission."

Mr. Behr led the way back toward the barn, but kept us hidden in the trees until they gave way to the field. I felt Steria before I saw her and pointed her out to Mr. Behr.

Coming in low to the ground, her crystalline scales sparkling in the late afternoon sun, she resembled a gorgeous, graceful bird. She beat us to the barn and swooped inside, a contagious urgency to her mood. We ran the last couple of yards and ducked inside the door. Mr. Behr was huffing and puffing, and I could tell his larger frame wasn't used to running. Steria was perched in the rafters.

Watch! her voice commanded.

Mr. Behr, and I poked our heads carefully around a window to peer out. The sight made me want to scream, but Steria whispered, *Shh!*

Professor Raleigh was following the driveway toward the barn. His machine was making the same steady beeping noise. Just as I was racking my brain for a desperate plan of escape, Chace's voice came hollering from back toward the house.

"Hey, mister!" A hunting rifle rested across his arms. "Watcha doin' on my property?"

The professor seemed taken aback. It was the first time I'd seen him at a loss for words.

"I asked ya what yer doin' on my property," Chace insisted gruffly.

Professor Raleigh seemed to gather his senses. "I was out bird watching."

"Well, I'm gonna have ta ask ya to leave. This is private property. If my dad finds ya, he won't be so kind."

The professor headed toward the river. "Thank you for the warning. I will head back to my vehicle."

"I'd advise ya to stay downriver. The further up ya go, the less friendly with strangers we are."

Chace walked behind the professor, and he soon left our sight. When Chace returned, he had a huge grin spread across his face.

"Do you think we scared him, Steria?" he asked out loud.

I do not know, Steria replied. *He will be back. He recognized you from Harley's house, but your weapon had him concerned.*

"I don't know how wise it was, Chace," Mr. Behr said, "But it was typical of the area, I suppose. Besides, I warned him."

"I know. Steria told me. That's why I did what Dad has always told me to if strangers come traipsing through."

"Steria told you?" I glanced between our dragon and my friend.

"Yep. She seems to know what we're all doing and can communicate with us when she's close enough."

Mr. Behr shook his head in amazement. "Well, why don't we stay here until the professor has a chance to make it a little ways down the road?"

"Steria," I said. "Can you do me a favor and head upriver during the day? I'd feel better knowing you're safe."

She nodded her head. *I can take care of myself, Harley, but I can do that if it makes you feel better.*

"I think it's a good idea," Mr. Behr surprised me by saying. "The farther away from people, the better you'll be. Adults won't understand or accept you like the kids have. They'll either want to dissect you and figure you out, or they'll fear you. I'm not sure which category Professor Raleigh falls into. I think the first. I do know his equipment doesn't have anything to do with geology."

CHAPTER 9: A FIELD TRIP

THURSDAY CAME BRIGHT and warm, perfect for a trip up the Rogue River. The traditional end of the year fieldtrip allowed the eighth grade class one last celebration by taking a jet boat ride. We enjoyed the hour long bus ride to the famous tourist attraction where we boarded the special boats designed to operate in shallow water. Once on the river, we jockeyed for the sides where a flat panel allowed us to lean over and trail our fingers in the wake without falling out.

"Alright students, are you ready for a unique trip thirty-two miles up the river?" our driver asked using the PA system from his position in the wheelhouse that spanned the width of the boat.

I sat next to Chace in the fourth row, about midway back, and joined the chorus of excited "yeses!" Cherise and Will looked over at me from the other side of the bench seat.

"My name's Boice, and that," he paused to point to the border collie that'd suddenly bounded onto the sideboard of the boat and licked Cherise, "is Aldyn. He's our mascot, and although he'd love to go up the river with us, will have to stay behind."

Groans met this statement. Boice chuckled.

"Don't worry, we'll keep you entertained. We'll be dropping the mail off as we go upriver, then we'll stop for a lunch break at the town of Brenton. On our way back, be prepared to get wet. I'll show you how maneuverable these jet boats are."

The trip was fun, and we saw some bald eagles and osprey. After about an hour of meandering through the river valley, Boice pointed out the hillside where bears could get blackberries later in the year. I thought I saw a purple bird and my heart sped up a beat. But there was no way that Steria could be down here. She was safely up Myrtle River back home. I pushed the thought from my mind.

By the time we reached the noon break, half the group was drenched from the three hundred sixty degree turns and hanging out the sides. We pulled into dock and enjoyed a delicious meal, purchased for us at the restaurant by the booster club. While the last stragglers finished their lunch, we had a little time to play, and most of us gravitated back to the river. Chace, Will, Cherise, and I wandered back toward the dock further upstream. As we moved away from the others, I felt Steria. I looked around, expecting to see her sparkling scales. I remembered the bird that I thought was our dragon.

"What are you looking for, Harley?" Will asked.

I shook my head. "I thought I felt Steria."

"You, too?" Cherise asked. "I thought it was just me."

I turned and stared at her. Her big brown eyes were as sincere as I had ever seen them.

"I thought I saw her earlier back on the river." Will's voice was tentative, as if he didn't want to admit it.

"Back where our driver pointed out the berries for the bears?" I gazed back down river.

Will nodded.

I called out in thought to Steria, but no reply came. I wasn't sure if I was glad or not. When I looked up, I saw Chace watching me through his bangs, his fingers wrapped around the logging suspenders his mother had given him.

"What's up, Chace?" I asked. "What do you know about this?"

A smile cracked his lips, and his eyes twinkled. "It was Steria's idea, but Mr. Behr agreed to it. She wanted to come with us. Mr.

Behr suggested she only come in on the wild section of the river where she was less apt to be seen."

"Except by us," Cherise said. "And thus, maybe by our whole class."

Chace shrugged. I shook my head and skipped a rock across the river. I wasn't sure I liked the idea of Steria being out here, yet at the same time, I didn't like the idea of her being alone on the ranch where Professor Raleigh would be able to get to her either. I shrugged.

"There's not much we can do about it now. Chace, do you know if she's still in the area?"

He nodded. "She had to head upriver because there's too many people around here. She'll follow us back down for a while and then head north over farm lands and the mountains back home."

"She's learned to fly," Cherise stated. I rolled my eyes, thinking she was stating the obvious. "No really," she insisted. "Steria could barely get out of the hayloft two weeks ago. Now she's flying this far from home. She's growing up."

I wondered what we were going to do with Steria. Obviously, a ranch wasn't going to provide the range she would need. We weren't going to be able to hide her for long.

CHAPTER 10: A HARD DAY'S WORK

IT WAS A hot summer. Normally the rains last until June, then the north wind blows. This year, we'd had no rain to speak of since April. The fire season signs had gone up before school was out. Most years, haying wouldn't start until after the fourth of July. That year, Chace's farm started to hay the week after school was out. Chace, Will and I were hired for the bucking crew. Karis drove Will and me out to the farm each day, and then my parents picked us up.

Lifting the bales from the ground onto the back of the truck, stacking them, and then unloading and restacking them in the barn was hard work, especially for me. Will and Chace had bulk to help them. I was still, as my mom so kindly put it, 'just waiting to fill out.' The other challenge I faced came from my asthma. Several times a day, I used my inhaler, but it was worth it. Although I was ready to collapse at the end of every day, we didn't call my folks to pick us up until after we'd stopped at the barn to see Steria. She greeted us eagerly each evening, either flying to meet us or nudging up against us. When she'd do that, my legs were so weak she'd knock me down. Then I'd get a face full of dragon muzzle.

"Steria, why can't you greet me more gently?" I asked one day as I stared up at a slobbery dragon mouth and tried to negotiate my back off the rock it had found when she knocked me over.

I received no reply, just a drip of dragon slobber on my chin.

"Ew!" I exclaimed, wiping it with the edge of my t-shirt. "That's disgusting!"

Meanwhile, Chace and Will were laughing.

"You should see yourself," Will said between giggles.

"Yeah, you look ridiculous!" Chace hid his laughter with a smile.

"Thanks. I can tell who my friends are here," I complained, trying to get Steria to back off.

Do you not like us, Harley? Steria asked.

I sighed and wrapped my arms around her scale-encrusted neck. "I love you, Steria, but I'm not so sure my friends appreciate how much more difficult this work is for me."

"Here he goes again," Chace said. "He's complaining about how small he is."

"But it's true," I protested.

"Oh, we know." Will sat down. "But by the end of the week you'll be stronger. You always whine at the beginning of track season, too."

I shrugged and then groaned as the muscles in my arms and shoulders let loose with their litany of complaints. I wished Steria would move just enough to let me up. As if in answer to my unspoken request, she shifted her weight, and I squirmed away from the rock.

"Come on, Steria," Chace called. "Give him a break. Let him up."

She moved, and I stood, leaning on Steria to help me rise. She now sat as tall as I stood.

We chatted amiably and joked around. Chace pulled some sodas out of a fridge. It was a perfect ending to the work day.

CHAPTER 11: A TENSE MOMENT

EVER SINCE I saw Professor Raleigh before school was out, I kept my eyes on the Seashore B&B when we passed. I wondered if he was still around.

One morning as Karis took me to the hay field, I glanced at the Seashore B&B. What I saw got my heart sprinting. Professor Raleigh and his pack were climbing into the white Taurus. Karis must have noticed my reaction.

"What's up, Harley? Are you scoping out the competition?"

I shrugged.

"All right, now," she said, adjusting her hands on the steering wheel as we turned up Myrtle River Road. "Out with it. You've looked over there every day as we go by, and today you jumped like you'd sat on a tack. What's up?"

Will shifted behind me but didn't offer any help. I didn't blame him. After all, she was my sister, not his.

"Did you see that man back there?"

"Yeah, he looked like the professor who stayed with us back in April."

"It was him," I agreed, and proceeded to tell her everything.

"You mean Chace actually met him with a shotgun?" Karis chuckled when I had finished.

"Yep," Will said. "I would've liked to see it."

Karis nodded as we rounded a curve. Then she asked, "Do you think he'll come back to Chace's place?"

"I don't know." I shrugged.

"But why?" Karis scrunched her nose thoughtfully. "Why would he want you guys to search for thundereggs if that's not what he was looking for?"

"I don't know." I drummed my fingers along my leg. "It's been bugging me too. Along with how he knows about her in the first place."

"*Does* he know about her?" Will asked.

"I guess we can't be sure." I stared out the window. "I always assumed he did, but I have no proof."

"Well, I'm going to keep my eye on him," Karis surprised me by saying. "You guys take care of Steria. I'll keep track of the professor."

*　*　*

The day dragged on. We had the bucking hay to do, but with monotonous work, it's easy to think of other things. My mind worked as hard as my arms, mulling over the problem.

At lunch, Will told Chace about seeing the professor. Chace's blue eyes took on a faraway look.

"Earth to Chace." I waved my hand in front of his glasses.

"I'm here. I was just checking on her. She's upriver and doing fine."

Will and I stared at him. A feeling of jealousy came over me. I wished I could have the same relationship with Steria that Chace had. But even setting that aside, there was still an apprehensive silence between us as we ate. How could we protect her?

The next four hours moved as slowly as molasses. Each row of hay bales loaded only revealed more to be gathered. Each tier that disappeared from the truck into the barn was only replaced by more of the green bales. But finally, the last bale was in the barn, and we were free for the evening. A half day of work remained. It was a bittersweet feeling. I was glad to be done so we could spend more time with Steria, but sad at the same time because there was no excuse to come up the river to be with her.

That night as we sat in the old barn sipping our sodas, we finally set about trying to find an answer.

"What if we moved her to some kind of national park?" I asked.

Will shrugged. Chace seemed lost in thought. I swirled the soda in my can. Finally, Chace looked up. His gaze rested on the young dragon, who was curled up in a ball nearby.

"There's another problem," Chace said. "The farmers upriver are losing cattle and sheep. They're blaming a cougar, but I'm not so sure. One of these days, she's going to leave a track, and we'll really have a problem on our hands."

The three of us looked to Steria, who rested serenely near our feet. She was such a sweet dragon, but she *was* a dragon. I was reminded of stories of kids who befriended cheetahs. It was fine when the cats were babies, but as they grew they were forced to release them into the wild. Our problem was that Steria didn't really belong anywhere.

With a sigh, I stretched and pulled out my phone. As usual, there was no reception.

"Chace, I'll need to use your phone."

He nodded. We got up and walked to the door, where a sound up the driveway caught our attention. Karis' car came into view, its nearly reckless speed leaving a cloud of dust in its wake.

"That's not good." I said dumbly.

"You're telling me." Will peered around my shoulder.

The car skidded to a stop and Karis stuck her head out the window.

"Where's Steria?" Her eyes roved the field.

I am here, the dragon's voice sounded in my mind.

I turned, as did Karis, to see Steria's purple scales sparkling in the evening light.

"Steria, you have to get out of here. The professor is coming with his machine. He's been up here all day, but just recently, he started moving, and he's coming this way."

We all looked to the river. What could we do? Chace's dad was home, but he didn't know about Steria. I looked around for inspiration and found nothing.

Steria seemed to understand the situation better than any of us. With a leap she was in the air and heading away from the river.

"Where's she going?" Karis watched her fade from sight.

I shook my head. "I don't know."

"She'll be all right," Chace assured us.

I wasn't so sure, and from the look on Will's face, neither was he. Chace herded us and Karis back to where we'd left our soda. He pulled out a can for Karis, and we sat and stared at each other, trying to think innocuous thoughts.

After about five minutes, the tension started to ease, since we all knew Steria had had plenty of time to leave the area. We made some attempt at small talk, but it wasn't the same without her. Footsteps sounded on the gravel outside, followed by voices.

"I don't know if you'll find what you're after, Professor," Chace's dad was saying. "There aren't a lot of lizards up here."

"Well, I thank you anyway, Mr. Martin." The professor's cultured voice slithered down my spine and set it prickling. "A scientist's job is to search all possibilities, even the faintest ones."

"What's your machine?" Mr. Martin's voice showed only minimal interest.

"It is a very special device. It uses satellite and thermal images to track any creature."

I shuddered at the thought, but didn't have a chance to do any more.

"Hey, Chace, boys," Chace's dad greeted us. "Oh, and Karis, isn't it? Nice to see you. Professor Raleigh, I'd like to introduce you to my son and his friends."

"Yes," the professor's voice dropped a few chilly degrees crisp as a fall morning. "We've met before. Haven't we?"

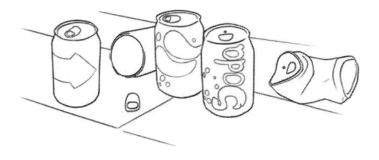

"Hi, Professor Raleigh," I said, my folks' training kicking in.

Karis seemed to have the same issue. "Hi, Professor Raleigh." She glanced to Mr. Martin. "The professor stayed at Aidan's Keep in April."

"Ah, yes," the professor agreed. "If I recall correctly, it was the boys' fault that my grant fell through. I was supposed to return to the college with a thunderegg, and the boys deprived me of it."

"I'm sorry you think that, professor." I looked up at the man from the floor where I sat. "But honestly, we didn't find a thunderegg."

"Yes, well, that is all past now. I am working on a new project. This time, I won't make the foolish mistake of involving mere children in my research." From the disgust in his tone, I expected to see him stick his nose in the air. "So, if you'll excuse me, boys, I am going to continue my search."

He turned toward the hayloft. Mr. Martin shrugged at Chace with a look that said he expected some answers from his son, then turned and followed the professor.

We sat back, but didn't relax. Our eyes followed the two men as they climbed the ladder, the professor toting his machine over one shoulder. We heard them moving around while hay filtered through the cracks in the hayloft floor.

The professor's voice trailed down to us. "These lizards are very elusive, Mr. Martin. It wouldn't surprise me if it lived here at night and roamed during the day. It wouldn't surprise me at all."

"I've never seen anything like you're describing, Professor, and I've seen my share of lizards around here."

"Yes, but rare ones seem to have their own habits, Mr. Martin."

I looked to Chace, who shook his head. We both knew Professor Raleigh was looking for a dragon, and kept our mouths very carefully closed.

Before long, the two men came back down the ladder. Once on the main floor, Chace's dad wiped his hands on his Carharts. The professor scanned the room.

"I thank you, Mr. Martin. If you don't mind, I'd like to return tomorrow morning and spend the day here."

"Well, professor, I leave at four thirty in the morning and don't get home until around noon. You've already said you don't want Chace messing things up; so the earliest you could come by would be one o'clock."

The professor looked as if he'd swallowed a lemon, and I took a gingerly sip of my soda to keep from laughing. He had worked himself into that one, and it served him right.

"I guess that will have to do, Mr. Martin. I am at the mercy of your schedule. I will see you at one o'clock tomorrow. Until then, I bid you good-eve."

As he walked out, we breathed a bit easier, but we knew we had barely beaten him this time. How long until we slipped?

CHAPTER 12: A TERRIFYING DREAM

"WHAT'RE WE GOING to do?" I exclaimed once Mr. Martin and Professor Raleigh's voices couldn't be heard anymore. "I can't take her to town again."

Karis' eyes grew wide. "You've had her in *town*?"

I nodded. "But only when she was an egg."

"Calm down, Harley." Chace pushed his hair out of his eyes. "She'll be okay. She'll come back tonight, and when Dad comes home, she'll leave and go up river."

"Are you sure it'll work?" Will said, voicing my own fears.

Chace stood. "Guys, we have work in the morning. There's not much we can do about it. We're going to have to let her be a big girl. She's been on her own all along."

"Yes." I slowly nodded my head. "But the professor hasn't been actively seeking her in her own home."

No one had an answer to that.

* * *

I didn't sleep well that night. I tossed and turned, and when I finally fell asleep, I dreamed.

The professor was chasing me, and I could see Steria just ahead of us. As I glanced back he took a device out of his bag, and a loud pop sounded. Ahead of me, Steria stumbled and went down. Another pop, and I saw the rope wrap itself around her muzzle. Her feet were caught in something like a net.

"No!" I screamed, tears running down my face.

My yell was drowned out by a third shot from the weapon Professor Raleigh held in his hand. A filmy white sheet landed on my face. It clung to my skin, and although I could hear Steria's struggle, I was blind. At the same time the sticky mess on my face began to draw tighter. It sank against my eyeballs, applying stinging pressure. Then it moved down my nose, encasing my nostrils. I scratched at it, but it wouldn't let go. I couldn't breathe! As soon as I took a deep breath through my mouth, the film entered, blocking all air.

I tried to scream again, but no sound escaped. Somewhere nearby I could hear Steria screeching, the sound raw and terrified.

"I have her, Harley, my boy." The professor's laugh filled my ears. "You will never see her again. Good-bye."

I awoke with a jerk, my breath coming in short, wheezing gasps. I felt along my nightstand for my inhaler. Groping in the dark, I found it and wrapped my fingers tight around the cylinder. My heart raced as I exhaled what little breath I had and then took a puff. As the medicine sped down into my airway I felt the constriction on my chest lessen, and finally my lungs opened to admit life-giving air. I sucked it in, all but panting in relief, trying to erase the last vestiges of the dream. A knock sounded on my door, and then it opened.

"Harley?" Karis' voice was barely above a whisper.

"Yeah?" My voice cracked.

"You okay?" She sat down on the edge of my bed. "Oh, not another asthma attack. Do I need to get Mom and Dad?"

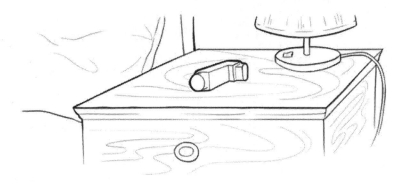

"No. I'm fine."

"You shouldn't have taken the haying job," she scolded me, but at the same time she rubbed her hand in circles around my back like she used to do when we were little and I'd have an attack.

I sat, still drawing in great draughts of air and trying *not* to think about the dream. My heart still raced.

"You screamed." The small circles continued. "That's not normal for an asthma attack."

"I had a dream, too." Minus Steria and the professor, it was a recurring nightmare. I blamed it on the asthma, which I'd had since I was little. It was like running a race and being winded, but instead of taking full breaths of air, trying to breathe through a half-clogged straw.

"Your suffocating dream?" Karis' voice was soothing.

I nodded. "This time Professor Raleigh was chasing Steria and me. He got us both."

Having said it, the power of the dream dissipated. My breathing, which had still been somewhat exaggerated and desperate, evened out as the tension faded.

"She'll be fine, Harley," Karis said. "If it'll make you feel better, we could call Mr. Behr and get help from him."

That sounded good. We were in over our heads, and probably should have admitted it sooner. I nodded.

"I'll call him before we go to work tomorrow." She just continued to rub my back. My eyes began to close.

"Thanks, Karis. I'll be okay now."

"You sure, little brother?"

"Yeah. Remember, I'm in high school now."

"Doesn't matter. You're still my little brother."

CHAPTER 13: A GREAT DAD

THE NEXT MORNING I dragged myself out of bed, motivating myself with the idea of talking to Mr. Behr. Just before seven thirty, I picked up the phone with a bit of trepidation; after all, I *was* calling a teacher at home *and* during summer vacation. I needn't have worried. His cheerful voice greeted me, and I wasted no time in explaining why I was calling.

"So, the professor has decided to explore the ranch, huh?" I could just see Mr. Behr standing with one hand on his belly and the other holding the phone.

"That's about right. Besides that, Steria's growing. She's getting hungry, and we're not positive she's not taking out local livestock."

"I'll see what I can do. I have a friend at UC Berkley in the biological sciences college. I'll ask her if she has any suggestions of where we could house a large predator."

After thanking Mr. Behr and hanging up, I rushed out the door. I didn't want to be late for my last day of work.

*   *   *

No matter how hard Chace had argued with his dad the night before, he hadn't received permission to follow Professor Raleigh around when he showed up. Nothing was stated about being in our barn though.

As soon as the last bale was safely stored in the hayloft, we ran back to the old barn and pulled out our lunches. It wasn't as much fun as when Steria was with us; plus we were rather nervous as well. We wondered what Professor Raleigh actually knew versus what he was just searching for.

Eventually, we reclined on our makeshift chairs from odds and ends we'd pieced together. I dozed off. The restless night along with the hard work made for a tired body. The professor's voice jolted me from my nap.

"Do you boys live in this barn?"

I looked up to see Mr. Martin fix him with an indignant gaze.

"Professor, my son lives on this land. He has every right to let his friends hang out here."

"Of course, Mr. Martin. Of course. It just caught me off guard to see them here again today. I thought I would be able to search without kids getting in the way."

Mr. Martin shook his head but didn't say anything

"I'll just begin upstairs and work my way down. I may have to disturb your rest, boys, when I get down here."

It seemed like Professor Raleigh was making fun of me, but no one would have been able to tell from his words or tone.

"That's no problem," I replied.

He nodded and moved on. Chace's dad glanced at us and then followed. Will rolled his eyes, and we all chuckled, relieving the stress a bit.

It seemed like forever before Professor Raleigh and Mr. Martin came down the ladder from the loft. When they did, the professor scoured the lower level, bending down, looking in the hay and placing anything from stray lint to small dirt clods in a bag. Finally, he made his way to where we sat.

"If you will excuse me, boys, I would like to see everything here, including the contents of your sacks." He pointed to our lunch bags sitting around.

"No, sir," Mr. Martin said irritably. "You've reached the limits of my patience and my hospitality. The boys' things don't have anything to do with lizards. You won't bother them. I'm sure any lizard would've skedaddled out of the way of being sat on."

The professor looked like he was going to argue, but one look at Mr. Martin's expression silenced any further complaints. Instead, he nodded and started poking around the rest of the room.

At the back of my mind, a question had been building, much like a wave out to sea. It started small and far off, easy to ignore, but now it had come crashing in on the shore of my mind. Before I could think better, I blurted it out.

"Professor Raleigh, when you first stayed at our house, you said you were a professor of geology."

"That's right." Chace nodded. "You were looking for thundereggs."

I picked up my question, glad Chace understood my thinking. "If you're a professor of *geology*, why are you searching for lizards? That would be *biology*."

Professor Raleigh straightened and seemed to tower over me, sprawled in the hay as I was.

"Very astute, my boy. Very astute. What you could not know is that certain creatures, especially lizards, need specific minerals to keep their metabolism going. Those minerals are found in specific *rocks*. I am still looking for rocks; I'm just using biological means of finding them."

He gave me an infuriatingly condescending smile that may as well have been the words: 'Don't bother; I have more intellect in my pinky toe than you ever will have.'

I must have made some noise of assent, because he finished the smile with a patronizing nod, then rummaged through the whole area. All the while he fussed and marveled over bits and pieces of things that appeared utterly insignificant. I couldn't fathom what an arbitrarily chosen bit of straw could tell him, but he put it in his bag with a lot of excited muttering. I suspected it was all staged for Mr. Martin's benefit, but I stayed quiet. Finally, he straightened up.

"Well, Mr. Martin, I believe I've found everything I can find here. I would like to search outside now."

"It's all right this once, with me along, I suppose," Mr. Martin said, "However, if you trespass on my property again, I'll call the cops. You've been rude to my son and inconsiderate of my time. So, today's it. Is that clear?"

Professor Raleigh seemed shocked. "I am ever so sorry, Mr. Martin. I meant no harm."

"That's my decision, sir. You'd best abide by it."

Inwardly, I cheered Chace's dad and something in my chest relaxed that I hadn't realized was tense. Steria's haven was secure again. Or at least, it was for as long as she could stay there.

CHAPTER 14: AN INDEPENDENCE DAY CELEBRATION

"HARLEY," MOM CALLED from downstairs that evening, "You have a telephone call."

I wrinkled my nose. Who'd call the house to talk to me? I shrugged and raced down the stairs. Mom's expression was one of curiosity and surprise, touched with a hint of suspicion. I shook my head to indicate I didn't know anything about the call. She shrugged and handed me the phone.

"Hello?"

"Hi, Harley, this is Mr. Behr. I heard back from my friend at the university."

Everything else around me no longer mattered.

"You did? What did you find out?"

"She doesn't know of any place to keep a predator, but she'll keep looking. She did tell me that Professor Raleigh may be a professor, but he doesn't teach anything at UC Berkley."

"*What*? But he said. . ." I trailed off.

Mr. Behr followed my trail and picked it up. "Exactly! He claimed to be a Professor of Geology at UC Berkley, but there's no professor, nor any students or former professors, with that name."

I stood staring blankly at the kitchen around me with its blue walls and the sun tea steeping on the windowsill.

"What now?" I finally managed to ask.

"Be very careful. I'd prefer that you kids not be around him at all."

I related what Chace's dad had mandated earlier that afternoon.

"That's good. I don't want you or Karis following him around."

I agreed. We chatted for a while longer and then said good-bye.

"What did Mr. Behr want, Harley?" Mom looked up from wiping the table as soon as I hung up.

"Chace, Will, and Cherise and I are still doing research with our project. Mr. Behr just wanted to check in."

"Since when does an eighth-grade project go into the summer?" Mom's hands on her hips showed her disbelief.

I shrugged. "We really got into it, and Mr. Behr said we could keep researching on our own if we wanted to."

Mom stared me down, but I held her gaze. At last, she turned away.

"You're up to something, Harley, but we've known Mr. Behr long enough to know he won't lead you astray. As long as Karis is with you *and* I know where you're at, I'm okay with this. The moment I find out it's dangerous, you'll be off the project like *that!*" She snapped her fingers.

I believed her. In our small community the rumor mill worked too well, and Mom could keep tabs on us more than we liked to admit.

*   *   *

I met Will the next morning at the crab shack and told him what Mr. Behr had told me. We were trying to figure out what to do when Cherise showed up. Of course, we had to fill her in on everything that had happened since school let out. Her dark hair brushed her shoulders every time she shook her head, as we told our tale. When we were done, she leaned back, crossed her arms, and stared out over the river.

"You know what I think?" When neither Will nor I answered, she continued. "Steria needs a home away from people where she can have access to food without stealing."

Will turned back to organizing lures on a shelf while I shared that Mr. Behr was looking into finding a place for Steria.

When I finished, Cherise changed the subject. "Are either of you going to be in the Fourth of July parade?"

I nodded. School sports wanted a float, and I'd agreed I'd be on it for track.

"Carl wants me to be on the crab shack float," Will said, referring to the business owner. "I get to throw the candy."

"Sounds fun," I grinned. "I'm just walking the parade route. What about you, Cherise?"

She shook her head. "Nope, not me. I get to collect candy. Maybe Chace will keep me company."

"Are either of you staying for the dinghy races or beach volleyball?" I asked.

"I can," Cherise said.

"Me, too." Will moved to a different set of lures to organize.

"Why don't we do the barbeque at the square and then hang out until the fireworks?" I suggested.

Cherise and Will agreed.

*　*　*

The parade had gone smoothly, and Cherise and Chace had picked up enough candy for themselves and Will and me to share.

The dinghy race was exciting, even though everyone knew who the likely winner was. Carl had convinced Will to join him as the third person on the crab shack's team, and they were first out into the waves, leaving the other two teams struggling against the breakers that pushed their dinghies sideways. The crowd cheered and shouted encouragement, but Carl was already halfway to the buoy by the time the others made it beyond the surf line. One boat, driven with powerful strokes by a guy who had the meatiest arms I'd ever seen, managed to make up the distance. He drew neck and neck with Carl's craft as they circled the buoy and came racing back toward the shore where their teammates were waiting to trade off. Will had waded waist-deep into the water, and the moment the bow was in reach, Will grabbed on and started working in tandem with Carl to get the prow pointed back out to sea. The surging waves made it hard going, but at last Will clambered aboard and took off for the buoy once more, still evenly matched with the second team. Will passed the third team as they came in, flying across the rough water even while they struggled with the exchange. "Look at him go!" I exclaimed to Cherise and Chace, who were watching just as intently as me. "He pulls as strongly as the grownups."

I was honestly impressed with my friend. Stroke by stroke, he pulled ahead of his competitor, giving a little breathing room to his last teammate. In a heart-pounding moment, we watched as the second team's boat capsized in the surf while they struggled to get back to the open water. The rower bounded back up, but the dinghy had already foundered in the waves. They had to drag the vessel up to the shore to empty it, and by the time they were back in the water, the third team had caught up with them and the crab shack's team was turned back toward shore.

Cherise was jumping up and down beside me, and I wasn't much more dignified. I was excited for Will. Normally, he's just a quiet guy with a shy smile, but when the final rower pulled in, he pretty much became a celebrity. The team celebrated as the crowd cheered. As we came up to Will, I overheard Carl exhilarating over their win.

"Will, you were amazing out there! I wouldn't fear handing you any of my boats. As soon as you turn sixteen, remind me to change your job description. I'll let you take people out crabbing."

"Thank you, Carl." Will looked at his bare feet in the sand, and I saw the red seep into his cheeks along with the telltale lines of a shy smile.

We whisked him away before he could be further embarrassed. We hadn't been able to get lunch yet, so we headed back up to the square where there were hamburgers and hot dogs for sale. Once we made it through the line and had greeted everyone from school, as well as all the community members who'd known us all our lives, we headed back to the beach to eat. The weather was perfect, no wind to speak of. I couldn't remember a Fourth of July in my fourteen years that hadn't been windy. The beach was crowded with people, both wading in the surf and playing or beachcombing on the shore. Shortly after we sat down, the teams formed up for volleyball, and we watched my dad drive home enough aces for me to have some bragging rights by proxy. I grinned and cheered him right through to the finals.

*   *   *

By the time people had gathered on the beach and the cliff behind it to watch the fireworks, we'd met up with my family. Mom had brought several blankets and sweatshirts for us to wear. Any other year I would've begged to have both, but this summer, I didn't need either of them. We all commented on how strange it was.

"Congratulations on winning the dinghy race," my dad told Will.

Will waved it aside. "It wasn't anything special."

Dad disagreed. "From what I hear, you rowed better than the adults. Carl says he wants you on his team every year, and he's trying to figure out a way to let you out in the boats this summer. He knows you're not old enough yet, but he's still scheming to get around it somehow."

Will shrugged bashfully; I knew he wasn't used to the attention. I wondered where his folks were. At least Chace's dad had greeted us before he left to sit with his own friends, but, as usual, Will's parents were nowhere to be seen. Cherise's mom and dad had stopped by the volleyball tournament and checked in with us, but they both had to work the next morning, so neither of them had stayed for the fireworks.

With the singing of the national anthem, I was sure we'd had the best Fourth of July yet. As the song wound to its spectacular end, which was punctuated by the first volley of fireworks, a sensation buzzed through my mind that I hadn't felt for several days. I tried to push it aside and just enjoy the evening, but it persisted. I noticed Will's head searching the skies, and not just where the fireworks were going off. Cherise's eyes were wide with wonder as she looked to the east away from the fireworks, but Chace had his head in his hands. My sister pointed to the east.

There, coming over the mountainside, was Steria. I groaned. *Why?* Her spread wings and serpentine neck covered what seemed like a gratuitously large portion of the sky. She paused before getting too close to the crowds sitting on the cliff and beach, but I could tell she was interested in what we were watching.

Go home! I thought toward her. As I did, I realized that was what Chace was doing: talking to Steria.

Another explosion in the air caught my attention, but not before I saw a red flame leap from Steria's jaws. As the flame spread away from her it turned to a vibrant purple that matched her amethyst scales, then faded into the night sky.

"Did you see. . .?" I asked.

Will nodded.

"She's a dragon after all," Cherise said, in her way of stating the obvious.

The next eruption of light was greeted by another splash of crimson and violet fire. Chace wasn't even trying to enjoy the fireworks show. In the light of the next volley I saw his hands pressed against his forehead, and for the first time in my fourteen years, I prayed for the show to be short, though I knew it to be futile. The citizens of Myrtle Beach loved their Fourth of July celebration and prided themselves on having a full hour of fireworks. Each explosion brought another splay of fire from our dragon.

The grand finale was a spectacular, brilliant, anxious nightmare. Steria sprayed her flames joyously, diving and barrel rolling through the air, and I ground my teeth and hoped that everyone else was too entranced with the lightshow to notice her. Once the last firework had faded from the sky, she finally turned and headed back to the mountain and up Myrtle River. I felt the reluctance emanating from her; she was overjoyed with her discovery, disappointed that her own celebration had been so brief, but I sighed with relief to see her go, then started wading into the annual chaos of people heading back to their cars. I wondered anxiously who else may have seen her cavorting through the night sky. She certainly hadn't been making much effort to be surreptitious.

Yawning a little as I mused, I wound through the trail that cut its way up the bluff when I bumped into someone. As I apologized, I looked up and recognized the face of Professor Raleigh.

"Harley," he greeted me. "Did you enjoy the show?"

I nodded, my heart in my throat and my voice offline.

"I especially enjoyed the purple and red ones," he said.

My mouth must have hung open. Karis, further up the path, turned and called, "Come on, Harley. Mom and Dad are waiting."

I nodded to the professor in a perfunctory show of politeness and took off, shaking.

When I caught up to Karis, she asked, "Anything to be worried about?"

I told her what'd happened.

"Oh no. What're we going to do?"

"I don't know."

I didn't like the sinking feeling in the pit of my stomach. We had to figure out something, and quickly. Odds were excellent that someone else had seen her, and the ensuing search could easily turn up her location, what with how big she was getting and all those missing animals. But where could she go?

CHAPTER 15: AN AFTERNOON UPRIVER

WITH CHACE UPRIVER without a driver's license and Will working at the crab shack, I didn't have anything to do. I roamed around town on my bike, pointedly avoiding Seashore B&B, hoping to avoid any further run-ins with Professor Raleigh. I was bored enough that I decided to swing by Cherise's house and see what she was doing. Just my luck—she wasn't home.

For lack of any other ideas, I headed over to the market, vaguely thinking that maybe I could get a sandwich. As I opened the door, the smell of hot dogs and homemade mustard filled my nostrils. The sound of the customers' chatter was dampened by the closely spaced shelves and the stuffed cougar, elk, and bobcat mounted on the walls and rafters.

"Hi, Harley," Stacey greeted me from behind the counter. "Here for some lunch?"

"Sure." I shrugged, then looked around and asked, "Where's your lunch rush?"

"You beat it, but not by much, I think. Give it a few minutes and we'll be busier than a bee."

I smiled. The market was known for its delicious deli sandwiches and hot dogs, both with a spicy, homemade mustard that gave them their signature taste. It wasn't uncommon for the lunch rush to last from eleven thirty until as late as four o'clock.

"So, what'll you have?" Stacey asked, already washing her hands.

"Hi, Harley," Ben, a friend from church called.

I waved, then turned back to Stacey and ordered the cranberry turkey sandwich. While she worked on it, I chatted with Jack, a life-time resident of the area. He was eating his lunch and shooting the breeze with the workers behind the counter. Laughter and joking filled the air. When my sandwich was ready, I sat down at one of the round tables in the small section between the frozen foods and the breads and crackers.

Halfway through my sandwich, Miss Smith passed me.

"Hi, Harley; how's your summer going?"

Around a mouthful of sandwich, I told her about the haying job and enjoying the Fourth of July.

"I saw that Will's team won the dinghy races," she said. "That was something to see!"

"Sure was," I smiled. "Been a bit dull since then, though. He's at work all the time."

"Ah, that's too bad, then," she said, sounding disappointed.

"Why?"

"I'd been planning to ask if you all would be interested in helping out at the country music festival. We need some extra people this year. Do you know if he ever gets any time off?"

"Oh, um, maybe. What's involved?"

"You'd be helping with parking, or guiding people across the road from the parking lot to the gate."

I shrugged, remembering how bored I was most of the time. Why not?

"When is it?"

"Two weekends from now. We'll meet with you on Thursday morning, and then you can get passes to the concerts as well."

I grinned. We all had been raised on country music, and I knew there were some big names showing up.

"Okay. I'll check with the others, but it should be fine with them. Even Will gets some time off on the weekends. Oh, but we don't have a ride, unless Karis can work as well."

"That'd be fine with me," Miss Smith said. "Karis would be a big help. They're expecting more people than last year, so like I said, we need the extra staff." Just then, Stacey called her to come pick up her finished order. As she walked away, Miss Smith turned over her shoulder and called, "Thanks so much, Harley. I'll see you there."

* * *

When I got home, Karis surprised me by offering to take me up to Chace's house. I gladly accepted, grabbed some old shorts for swimming, and hopped in the car. As we rounded the curve at Cabbage Creek campground, I spotted a white Ford Taurus sitting in the day use parking lot. Karis must've seen it at the same time I did, because I felt the car slow, but she continued on. At the next driveway, she pulled the vehicle to a stop. A cattle gate blocked the way back into the field; a large padlock and chain added to the deterrent to any trespassers.

"Come on, Harley. Let's go."

I looked at her blankly. She waved for me to get out of the car. I shrugged and did as she suggested. Mr. Behr's warning about the professor nagged at my thoughts like a persistent mosquito, but I ignored it and followed my sister.

"Harley, look at those plates."

Karis pointed to the license on the Taurus. They were government plates! How had we missed that before?

"Do those mean the professor is working for the state?" I asked.

"Not necessarily," she said thoughtfully. "The school busses have government plates, too."

I nodded, but then thought of something. "But usually the school vehicles have state plates and say publicly owned. These say US Government."

Karis' eyebrows raised. "Maybe then, but I don't know."

Suddenly Mr. Behr's warning sounded like fantastic advice.

"We need to know what he's up to, though." Karis stepped up to the car and looked in. She tried the handle, but the door was locked. "Look, Harley." She pointed with her finger against the window.

I pressed my face to the window and used my hand to shield the glare of the sun. What I saw blew my mind. The back seat was filled with all kinds of electrical equipment. Boxes, LCD screens, and meters of all sizes were packed into the space. I whistled, but it was cut short when I saw a symbol that I'd only seen in movies.

"Karis," I whispered in awe. "Look at that."

"Let's go, Harley. We can't deal with this on our own."

I nodded, mute, and the silence followed us all the way back to the car. The thud of the doors and the snick of seatbelts only seemed to punctuate it. Karis placed her hands on the steering wheel, staring straight ahead, too still for comfort. After several minutes, she started the engine and put the vehicle in gear.

Not a word passed between us while we wound upriver to the old barn, even after Karis put the car in park and killed the engine. We sat for a while, the clicking of the cooling car barely registering in my ears while we stared unseeing at the dry fields.

Harley? Karis? Steria's voice was barely more than a whisper in my mind. *What is wrong?*

I looked to Karis, but she just shook her head helplessly. So I answered, "Remember how we told you about Professor Raleigh Well, we now know he isn't working for a university. He's a government agent."

Why does that scare you, Harley?

How could I explain it to her? Images from all the science fiction movies I'd ever seen with aliens and government officials flashed through my mind. My dream with the professor and his net gun came back in full clarity.

He will do this? Never before had fear tinged Steria's words. She'd always seemed confident and in control.

I nodded, pained that she'd sensed all that. "Maybe more."

Then we had best make sure he doesn't find me. Steria gained back some of her usual bravado.

* * *

We spent the morning with Chace and Steria, trying to relax at the barn and watching her fly, but there was a pervasive sense of unease that everyone was trying not to talk about. I expected Professor Raleigh to show up, waving some badge and demanding we hand Steria over to him. After a lunch I couldn't remember tasting, we decided to try going swimming with Steria, but the malaise clung to us, so instead we skipped rocks and walked along the shore for a while. Eventually, when Steria went hunting, we did get in the water, and it seemed like the flowing water carried away some of the cloud we had been feeling. Before long we were splashing and having a good time, and the symbol we had seen seemed a mere distant memory.

"Harley James!" Karis yelled. I grinned and scooped up another handful of water, laughing at her already dripping eyelashes. Her eyes filled with fire, and I instantly abandoned any plan of a second attack. I dove into the river with Chace right behind me. She shook her head with her hands on her hips. She reminded me of Mom. I didn't dare say that, though. Suddenly, I saw her expression change, registering the sort of fear that I normally associated with baseless accusations and unfair authority figures. Slowly, I looked over my shoulder. Standing on the far bank was the professor, a full frame Nikon holstered on one hip, a beeping gadget on the other. He looked extremely unhappy and agitated as he walked to the edge of the water. "Why do I keep running into you kids?"

I shrugged.

Chace wiped water from his face. "Maybe because you keep coming to my home. Remember what my dad told you last time you were here?"

"I'm by no stretch of the imagination anywhere on your property. From my research, this side of the river is BLM land. There's nothing you can do about it. Nothing at all."

"Just make sure you stay on that side of the river then," Chace said.

"Don't worry, I will. But when I do come back, I'll have every legal right on my side."

A shiver ran over my body. I wanted to blame the wind that blew up the river valley, but I knew better.

With a wave of his hand, the professor—no, the agent, as we now knew—turned and walked away from the river.

CHAPTER 16: A MUSIC FESTIVAL

"COME ON, HARLEY," Karis called. "Get up. We need to be at the festival by nine."

I turned over and groaned. The dream had returned last night and brought another asthma attack along for the ride. I took a deep breath and hauled myself out of bed. I really was looking forward to the festival; it'd be the first time since the fireworks that we'd all be together. I didn't even mind having Karis there with us. Most kids would think it was weird, but with all that'd happened with Professor Raleigh and Steria, Karis was as much a part of the group now as the rest of us, big sister status notwithstanding.

Mom had fixed french toast—my favorite—and Karis and I made some amiable small talk with the other guests at the breakfast table. I was reminded of that early morning conversation with Professor Raleigh back in April. As I chewed, I wondered what the government wanted with Steria. No good ideas came to mind, and I passed most of the rest of the meal in a nervous silence. Clearing the table, we bid our guests good day.

Karis picked up Will and Cherise on our way out; Chace had a ride with a neighbor. The music festival grounds were rented from a local rancher. Music lovers camped in their fancy RVs and walked from their miniature homes on wheels to the actual concert arena. Miss Smith had left a parking pass for us at the market, so the man directing traffic waved us on to the parking lot for vendors. I hadn't been to the festival before and was thoroughly impressed with the layout and manpower involved. More volunteers guided us to our parking spot, then pointed us in the direction of the gate where we'd meet our supervisor.

As we walked, country music filled the air from a hundred different speakers, all playing different songs for the people in range of each individual sound system. A tractor with a trailer holding long benches rumbled past, filled with people going from parking to the concert area. Beneath its wheels, we could see the larger version of the billowing dust clouds that sprang up under every step we took. The sun beat down relentlessly despite the early hour, and I wished I'd brought a hat.

More volunteers directed us across the road to an open field where pavilions created the gates for entrance to the concert itself. Another long tent held tables filled with small boxes holding wristbands and other miscellaneous supplies. A large screen TV broadcasted the happenings on the stage somewhere off in the distance, but there wasn't much going on yet besides a few sound technicians and gofers going over the setup.

A lady behind one of the tables motioned us to her.

"You kids volunteers?"

"Yes, ma'am," Karis greeted her. "Miss Smith with the school told us about it."

The lady nodded, bent over, and brought some t-shirts out of a box she had next to her.

"Here you go: One for each of you, and let me get your bracelets..." she rifled around in another box as we pulled the t-shirts on over our own.

She came up with several nylon bands and fastened one on each of our wrists. "Now, don't pull it too snug," she warned. "The clasp is only designed to slide tighter. The bracelet is your ticket for the weekend to any of the concerts. Give me a minute to get Zach; he'll let you know what you're doing."

We nodded and adjusted the bracelets to a comfortable length, looking around and orienting ourselves in the enormous space. Spread out before us was a sloped field, with the stage nestled at the bottom. The vendors' tables flanked the approach to the stage and circled around the seating areas, and I smelled the beginnings of carnival food and other dishes coming from my left. Before long, Zach showed up and led us to the gate. He put a scanner in each of our hands and directed our attention to the barcode on each bracelet.

"Scan every person before letting them continue to the security check point. If you have a problem, just wave, and I'll come help you out."

*   *   *

The next four hours passed without any problems. It was a bit monotonous, but at the same time fun. I saw a bunch of people that I knew, so we chatted as they waited to pass through the security check. Finally, I was given a break and a lunch voucher, which I took gratefully.

Zach had told me that both the Rotary Club food booth and the clam chowder booth had the best meal choices. As I tried to decide which to do, a friendly voice greeted me. I turned to see Mr. Behr.

"Hi, Harley, how's your summer going?"

"Busy. I'm helping at the gate today with the others."

He nodded. "I saw Cherise. How's our project going? Is she okay?"

I understood that his cryptic questions referred to Steria, and I nodded. "I need to talk with you about it, but I don't get off for another four hours. Can we chat then?"

"Sure. I'm here all day."

The next four hours seemed to drag by. More people moved through my line, an endless motley of faces and bracelets. At last, Zach came and collected my scanner.

"Still willing to do this tomorrow, Harley?"

I grinned and wiped a hand across my forehead for the thousandth time. "Sure, as long as it doesn't rain."

He laughed. "With the summer we've had, I really doubt it. Any other year, and I'd say I'd need to find a new volunteer."

"See you tomorrow, then."

I met up with the others inside the gate. Music was blaring from the large speakers as Thompson Square sang. I wanted to find a quieter spot to call Mr. Behr. Before I could tell anyone about meeting him, Karis grabbed my arm and turned me around.

"What—" I exclaimed, but there was no way she heard me over the song.

Karis put her ear to mine. "Look over there. It's Professor Raleigh. He doesn't exactly blend in with the country music fans."

I turned to look where she had pointed. Sure enough, the professor stood out like a hunter's orange vest in the forest. He wore khaki dress pants with a red polo shirt; everyone around him was in blue jeans, button up plaid shirts, and cowboy hats and boots or Romeos. He was facing away from us and heading toward the food vendors.

"Come on, guys," Chace hollered over the noise. "We've got to find out what he's after."

"Wait!" I surprised myself with the force of the command. "Let's call Mr. Behr first."

"Why?" Cherise scrunched her nose.

"I saw him when I went on break. He's here and wants to meet with us. Maybe he can help."

I fumbled with my phone, trying to dial the number. Once I had that accomplished, it was another hassle just trying to hear. I plugged one ear and held the phone to the other. By the time I'd explained everything to Mr. Behr, we'd lost the professor in the crowd. Chace was hopping mad, but I tried to calm him.

"You saw how he's dressed, Chace. No way we could lose him for long."

"Right, Harley." Sarcasm dripped from his words. "There's only fifteen thousand people here. How're we going to find him?"

"Just like we've found everyone else we know. He's bound to show back up."

Chace shook his head. We all headed in the direction Professor Raleigh had gone. Somewhere between the coffee shop, the Rotary Club's burger shack, the Chowder House, and other smaller food vendors, Karis spotted him. He was chatting with someone I didn't recognize.

"Who's that?" Will stood on tip-toe to see better.

I shrugged. The two seemed deeply immersed in their discussion. They didn't see another larger man back up to them, and so they weren't able to avoid colliding with him as they turned. At the impact, the man lost his grip on his cup, and it sailed up in the air to land at the feet of Professor Raleigh and his conversation partner, splashing bright red punch liberally over the man's jeans.

Cherise's gaped, and Karis held her hand over her mouth, fighting not to laugh. I couldn't help but let a giggle escape. Mr. Behr had found the professor first.

"...so sorry." A lull in the music allowed us to hear Mr. Behr. "Here, let me help."

He proceeded to ineffectively use several napkins to clean up the mess.

"Sir," Professor Raleigh said, but when Mr. Behr didn't stop, he repeated it. "Sir, please, I'm sure my colleague can clean this up on his own."

Mr. Behr straightened up. "Why, hello. It's Professor Raleigh, right?"

The professor paused, a quizzical expression on his face. "Do I know you?"

"We met up Myrtle River back in May. You were looking for rocks at the time, I believe. I'm Mr. Behr, local science teacher."

The professor's face registered a guarded recognition. "Ah, yes. Yes, I remember. You gave me warning about traipsing up along the river. I thank you for that. It kept me from being accosted with shotguns."

"I'm so glad I could be of help. Did you find those thundereggs you were looking for?"

We inched forward to hear as the music on the stage started back up. The professor had his back to us, and Mr. Behr was studiously ignoring us.

Professor Raleigh's face twisted in disgust. "No, I was stupid and didn't do all the research myself. I enlisted the help of some teenagers, and they stole my find. They claim they never saw it, but I don't believe them."

"I'm so sorry to hear that. I'm sure you did the best you could; you couldn't know they would make off with it. Besides, even the best scientists have helpers with their research."

"Why, thank you for your kind words, but really, I am sure you don't want to spend your time chatting with me. You came to a concert to enjoy the music."

The professor edged away, but Mr. Behr raised a hand.

"Actually, Professor Raleigh, it's much more enjoyable over here where I don't have my eardrums blown away. Who's your friend?"

Me. Behr turned to the other man. "You seem familiar, but I can't place where."

"I'm with the South Coast Search and Rescue."

"Oh, then you must just look like someone I know. Anyway, what brings you here, Professor?" Mr. Behr asked. "Do you like country music?"

The professor laughed, almost a bark. "Hardly. Actually, this place may hold a key to my current research."

"Which is?"

Professor Raleigh looked to his left and right, then shrugged. "Seeing you are a man of science, I suppose I can tell you. I have a theory that it's possible to discover animal life by following geological signs." When Mr. Behr leaned in to hear more, the professor continued. "You know certain stones and rocks contain minerals. Those minerals can be traced to specific needs in animals. So, where those minerals exist is where those animals will be found. I think I'll have some luck here, and, of course, I'd never be allowed on the ranch grounds if there wasn't a concert going on."

Mr. Behr nodded. "That sounds reasonable. What creature are you looking for?"

"A special lizard."

"Well, there are all kinds of lizards around here. I hope I don't have to warn you of the salamanders—I once knew a man who had one attack him. It was far more severe than you might think; he had more than a few stitches by the time it was all done." Mr. Behr's expression showed how serious he was.

I glanced to Will and Chace, who both rolled their eyes. We'd heard that story so many times, but the professor didn't seem to mind.

"I have dealt with many different lizards. I will be very careful with this one."

"I'm sure you will." Mr. Behr moved his hands in a calming manner. "Thank you so much for chatting with me."

Karis pulled my arm and grabbed Chace. We turned and walked over to the other side of one of the food booths, Will and Cherise tagging along. After a few moments, Mr. Behr joined us, but the music was particularly loud at the moment, so instead of trying to converse right away, we purchased some food and sat down at a free table a little farther away from the stage.

"So, what information did you want to talk to me about, Harley?" Mr. Behr took a bite of his hamburger.

I explained all I had seen in the professor's car up at Cabbage Creek campground.

"It wasn't until I saw the emblem on the back of one of the monitors that I got worried." I sipped my Coke. "It's of a squat eagle with its wings spread out. I knew I'd seen it before. When I got home, I looked it up. It's the symbol for the NSA!"

The others sat staring at me, but Mr. Behr nodded.

"I'm glad it scared you away. I don't know what Raleigh is really up to, but one thing I do know is he's not safe for you kids to be around him on your own. He's already said repeatedly how he doesn't like you, and if he's NSA he could have resources to help him remove you from the equation, legally or otherwise."

"But, Mr. Behr," Chace said as he licked a bit of ketchup off his fingers, "If he comes around Steria, I'm going to take him on."

"I know, Chace. I just hope it doesn't come to that."

We ate our meal without any further discussion, occupied by the music and commotion around us. When we were done, we all went over to the stage area, where the grassy slope was already filling up with people for the evening concert. Florida Georgia Line was scheduled to take the stage shortly, but during the interim, canned music filled the air. The song "Come On and Dance with Me" came on. Karis stood up, grabbed me and began dancing and singing to the song. I shrugged, helpless. The boys laughed at me until Cherise stood and pulled Will to his feet. His face was beet red.

I laughed. "Will, your face looks as bright red as a hunter's jacket."

"Thanks, Harley; that's exactly what I needed to hear."

"I'm just glad it's not me," Chace said to Mr. Behr, who laughed his deep belly laugh.

Karis grinned, winked at me, and turned to Chace.

"Oh, no, you don't," he protested, but she pulled him to his feet. "I don't know how to dance."

"Just don't let her step on your toes, that's all!" I called.

He shook his head and gave in to the inevitable.

It was nice to forget about our worries for a while. I looked forward to the next couple of days—eight hours of scanning was a small price to pay for evenings like this.

CHAPTER 17: A RELAXING AFTERNOON

THE DAY AFTER the music festival ended, I slept in. It was so nice to relax. When I woke up, I meandered down to the dining room. All the guests had already had their breakfasts, so I wandered into the kitchen and helped myself to some cereal and milk. Halfway through my bowl, Karis joined me.

"Any plans for today, Harley?"

I shrugged. "Relax."

She grinned. "I hear you. I don't want to do much either. What about a swim at Cabbage Creek Campground?"

I eyed her. "That's relaxing?"

"Yeah, as long as we don't meet anyone. Besides, we can swing by and see Chace if you want."

I nodded. "Sure. Bring the others?"

"If they can come."

Suddenly, my day off sounded more like a day of activity than recuperation.

I called Will first. He was at the crab shack working. Cherise was available, so we picked her up and headed upriver. No Ford Taurus greeted us as we passed Seashore B&B. I wasn't sure if that was a good sign or not. The campground parking lot was free of any suspicious looking cars as well, though I did see a pickup with a search and rescue sticker.

The water was just right. We splashed around, swimming and playing for a couple of hours. As the sun climbed higher, Karis was the first to get out and sit on the shore. I soon joined her and began skipping rocks, and before long Cherise sat down next to me. The sound of the rippling river filled the air. A bird sang nearby.

Occasionally, a cow would low somewhere in the distance. My rocks added a percussion to the rhythm of the river bank as they skidded across the water and then fell with a plop to sink to the bottom.

"I wonder what it's like to fly." Cherise's comment interrupted the flow of our surroundings.

I glanced at her, confused as to where the idea had come from, but with Cherise, that was par for the course. She often had thoughts from left field.

"Do you feel free and light, or is it like you're going to fall all the time?"

"Okay, now *that* would be terrible." I shook my head. "I don't think it's the last one. Why would anything continue to fly if they felt like they were going to fall?"

"I don't know." Cherise shrugged her shoulders. "I just wondered."

I thought Karis was asleep, but she surprised me, though she kept her eyes closed as she lay on her towel. "I think it's the first one, Cherise. You don't have any fears and everything is just free."

I shrugged. It made sense. "Why don't we ask Steria the next time we see her?"

"Let's go now." Cherise jumped up and begun to gather her things.

Karis slowly stretched and sat up. "What do you think, Harley?"

"Sounds good."

Within five minutes, we were at the old barn on Chace's place. He wasn't there, and neither was Steria.

"What now?" Karis looked around peeking her head out the main door.

I paused. *Steria?* I called in my mind. *Are you anywhere near the barn?*

I couldn't feel her presence, but I had the sense that she was close. I sat down and wondered where she could have gone. A picture of the river as if from a drone's camera came to my mind. The river flowed lazily by, its liquid green highlighted by sparkles from the sun. The trees rushed underneath, waving under the weight of the north wind. A tight turn and suddenly, I was looking in the other direction. Another turn and my stomach began to heave. The picture vanished and I was sitting on the floor in the barn.

"You okay, Harley?" Cherise looked at me with her big eyes full of concern.

"I think I am. I'm not too sure after that."

Karis looked like she was about to puke. "You too?"

I nodded, but the nausea was too much. "Yes."

Cherise grinned. "I think we have the answer to what it's like to fly."

"I was fine until the sudden turns." I wiped my mouth with the back of my hand.

"Well, in that, you are truly my brother," Karis agreed.

A knock at the door stopped our conversation. "Hello?"

I got to my feet. "Yes?"

"Oh, hey," a man said, as he rounded the corner and saw us. "I was wondering if there was anyone around. I'm looking for the owner."

I stared, amazed. The man was the same one that'd been with Professor Raleigh at the music festival, the one who'd said he was in search and rescue.

"I don't know if Chace's dad is around right now." Karis stepped forward. "We're his friends and came to see him. How can I help you?"

The man looked down from his six foot four height. His expression was almost sour. I wasn't sure if he didn't like us being here or if he thought Karis was ugly. His brown eyes took us in and then softened.

"Well, I'm on the South Coast Search and Rescue Team. We have some training coming up and are looking for a place with hills, woods, river, and wilderness to use as our training grounds. The ranches up this way are perfect for that sort of thing."

It sounded reasonable. If this was the first I had met him, I'd have had a totally different reaction, but knowing he was with Professor Raleigh made me want to kick him out the door.

Karis was more diplomatic. "Do you have a business card? I could give it to Mr. Martin when he gets in."

The man nodded, and gracefully reached into his back pocket. His smooth motions reminded me of an actor I'd seen on Mission Impossible. He was every bit the international spy, complete with good looks and nice manners. I looked for the tale-tale signs of a concealed weapon, but couldn't find any. It wouldn't have surprised me, though. He pulled out a worn leather wallet with some bills sticking out the edges. The wallet was thick with business cards, credit cards, an ID card, and other papers. He handed Karis a card with a picture of a German shepherd and some sort of seal on it.

"You can have him contact me at that number."

"Okay, um…" She checked the card. "Bryan."

"Were you kids at the country music festival?"

My heart sped up, but then I remembered that fifteen thousand people were at that festival.

Karis nodded. "Yeah, we were volunteers."

"I thought I recognized you." He smiled. "Well, I'd better get going. I'm staying at Cabbage Creek Campground right now. I'll check my voice mail and email regularly to hear back from—Mr. Martin, you said?" He waited for a nod from Karis, and then he waved and turned.

"He was cute," Cherise said.

"Yeah, but more importantly, he's working with Professor Raleigh," Karis said. "And now we have his contact information."

"So, what now?" Cherise asked.

"We do some research." Karis tapped the card against her other hand. "Let's head home and look him up online. I could also call the search and rescue place and see if they've heard of him."

* * *

The afternoon didn't yield much. We discovered that Bryan Taylor did indeed work with the South Coast Search and Rescue. He also was known for smoke jumping in the summer. That probably explained his presence in the area right now; the fire season was in full swing, and the warning level had risen two levels since May. We had no clue what exactly his involvement with Professor Raleigh entailed.

* * *

Steria bumped up against me. I rubbed her hard, scaly head. The light refracted off her scales, making them sparkle like the jewel she resembled. I smiled. Then I heard the sound I'd feared. I jumped at the explosion.

"Run, Steria!" I yelled as I turned to face the threat.

Professor Raleigh stood with his feet planted and his device in his hand. His other held a badge.

"Harley, you can't fight the government for long. Surrender her before people are hurt. I just want to get her to a safe place where she can't hurt anyone."

Steria hurt someone? Never!

"I know what the government does to creatures they've never seen before! Ever watch *E.T.?* That's not going to happen to Steria!"

"You're wrong, Harley. I won't let them do anything like that to her. Remember, I'm a scientist. I want to protect life."

"Right." My voice was thick with sarcasm. "And biologists don't dissect animals, right?"

I glanced over my shoulder to see Steria still there.

"Run!" I told her. She just stood there, looking at me.

In slow motion, I saw the professor raise his device to firing level. Then I realized why she hadn't run. A sticky web clung to her feet. I tried to run to her to help her, but the explosion sounded again. The next moment, the clinging substance was attacking my eyes.

"No!" I tried to scream, but nothing came out.

Another pop, and the film filled my nose and then my mouth. I tried to gasp for air, but none came. My hands began to flail, tearing at the sticky mess covering my face. My brain screamed at me to breathe.

* * *

Blankets crawled around my face. I sat bolt upright in bed, wheezing. With slow movements, I reached for the inhaler. It wasn't where I normally put it. I groped in the dark until my hand landed on it. A small puff of air escaped my lungs, and then the life-giving aid of albuterol filled them. I sat panting, my heart racing as I fought my way out of the last clinging panic of the dream. It was the nightmare again.

I lay back down, but my mind raced. There was no way I was going to be able to sleep any time soon.

CHAPTER 18: A WORRISOME PROBLEM

"HARLEY," KARIS CALLED the next morning. "Get up."

I groaned and covered my head with the blankets. She knocked again, more insistently this time.

"Go away!"

I heard the door open. "Come on, Harley. Get up."

I sighed and pushed the covers away from my face. "Why?"

"Because we're going to find out what Professor Raleigh is up to once and for all."

That got my attention. I nodded. As soon as she shut my door, I swung my feet over the edge of the bed and stretched. I threw on a T-shirt and pulled up some shorts. The day already promised to be warm—I'd slept with my window open, and it was pleasant in my room.

Once I made it downstairs, Karis handed me a bowl of cereal and a cup of coffee. At my astonishment, she replied, "You look like you could use something to help wake you up."

I nodded my thanks since my mouth was full of puffed wheat. I took the food to the table where Mom expected us to eat. Once there, Karis started to share her ideas.

"Professor Raleigh has to be somewhere online. If we can find him, we'll have a better idea of what he's doing. I also thought I'd go chat with Mary at Seashore B&B and see what she knows about him."

I wondered if I'd heard correctly. It was standard practice to *not* divulge guest information to others, and Mary was a stickler for rules.

"How'd you plan on doing that?"

Karis smiled enigmatically. "I have my ways. Besides, I have the phone number of the professor's acquaintance. I'm sure he would need Bryan's contact info. So, I'll go to Mary and explain I have information that one of her guests needs."

I shook my head, not following my sister's logic, and focused on eating. Karis was apparently fine with that.

"I want you to do the internet research while I go talk with Mary. Can you handle that?"

I nodded. "I don't know what I'm supposed to find out since Mr. Behr already tried and didn't discover anything."

"I know." Karis ruffled my short hair. "But I think you'll find something. Maybe search his name and fantasy creatures or dragons. Who knows?"

I shrugged. "Doesn't hurt to try."

I put my dishes in the dishwasher and headed to the computer upstairs. My folks didn't believe in letting kids have their electronics in their own room, so our family had a computer that sat in the hallway between all the rooms. The guests could use it if they needed, but it was mainly for the family.

I sat down and typed in *Professor Winston P. Raleigh fantasy creatures biologist* and waited for Google to respond. The first link was an educational journal written by a Professor Winston; the second was a newspaper article about Bigfoot. I shrugged and opened them both in new tabs. I couldn't understand much of the first article, but when I scrolled to the bottom there was a picture of Professor Raleigh looking back at me. The biography indicated that the professor was an adjunct professor of biology at the University of Iowa. I frowned—that didn't make sense. Then I glanced at the date. The article had been written five years ago.

The Bigfoot piece was easier to understand, being written with all the hype of a tabloid paper. A Bigfoot sighting in northern California was the object of discussion. Several people claimed to have seen Bigfoot somewhere in northern California, and the text was flanked by a grainy photograph showing a big, hairy creature that was somewhere between an ape and a human. One of the people interviewed was a Professor Patterson who said the creature should be given sanctuary in a home away from humans where it could be safe and live in peace. I re-read those words. They sounded very similar to the professor's words in my dream. I shuddered. As I scrolled further, there was a picture of Professor Patterson, looking decidedly familiar. I shook my head; how many different names did Professor Raleigh go by?

I went back to my Google search and typed in *Professor Winston Patterson Raleigh NSA*. The first hit took me to a newspaper article. The professor was at the bottom of the page, listed as special agent on assignment in the US. I sat back in my chair and stared at the picture of the professor. *What type of special assignment?* I wondered. No amount of searching gave me any more information. I hoped Karis had better luck than me.

*   *   *

Karis returned without much new information. She'd learned that the professor had registered with the name Winston P. Raleigh. He'd given an address from California and said he worked for UC Berkley. Karis was impressed with what I'd found, but it didn't tell us really much more than we already knew.

"What now?" I asked.

Karis fiddled with the business card. "Should I call Bryan?"

I shrugged. "What good would it do us? It could get you in trouble."

"I guess you're right." She pocketed his contact information, frowning. "I just think we should do something."

I nodded. "But what?"

Neither of us knew. With a sigh, I headed to my bike. I could ride around town looking for the professor, although I doubted it would help us any. But still, it was better than nothing, right?

Maybe, but a few hours later I'd proved myself correct, with exactly zero sightings of Professor Winston Patterson Raleigh. I ended up at the beach, watching the waves wash along the shore. As the afternoon wore on, I headed to the market. Maybe I could hear something there. It was the place where everyone came to catch up and pass the time with idle chatter and gossip

I ordered the famous hot dog complete with pickles and homemade mustard. While Stacey was fixing it up for me, I grabbed some salt and vinegar potato chips and a lemon lime soda to go with it. After thanking Stacey, I sat down to eat and listen.

As was customary, Stacey and the others had their hands full keeping up with the lunch rush. The conversation of customers filled the air, along with orders being called. I sat enjoying it all and greeting friends as they came by. I was sipping the last of my soda when I overheard a conversation at a table nearby where two ranchers were talking.

"What do you make of Robert's idea of what's getting the lambs upriver?" Tony Watson, who had one of the largest sheep ranches in the area, asked his friend. I recognized Tom Longton, another sheep rancher upriver from Chace's place.

Tom snorted in response. "Of all Robert's crazy ideas, that one takes the cake."

"But he claims he saw it and got a photo."

"A photo of a *dragon*? If you believe that, Tony, you'll believe anything!" Tom wiped his mouth with a napkin and started gathering the garbage from his meal.

"I know, it sounds outrageous, but if dragons *did* exist, it'd make the most sense to those killings." Tony took a drink of his soda.

Tom sat back in his chair. "I don't know." He shook his head, greeted someone as they walked by, and then stared into space. "I saw a kill. The grass was gone around the lamb and nothing was left but bones. The ground looked burnt. Cougars don't leave a kill; they drag it off somewhere. Coyotes'll leave some of the lamb, but they kill at the throat and bite the hind legs."

Tony nodded. "I still think it's crazy, but I'm about ready to listen to far-fetched ideas. I've lost too many lambs and ewes up that way."

Tom gathered his trash together. "Me, too. I need to go make sure everything's fine at my place. It was good to see you, Tony."

"You too, Tom." Tony downed the last of his soda and rose.

I sat stunned. I'd known Tony and Tom all my life. They were sane men, simple, honest ranchers. If they were seriously thinking a dragon was responsible for the livestock kills, then we were in trouble.

*   *   *

I didn't want to go home right away. Instead, I hopped on my bike and headed to the crab shack. I hoped to find Will and convince him to agree to a sit down with everyone. I was in luck. Will was eating lunch when I arrived. I explained about the conversation I'd overheard.

"We have to do something," I said.

He nodded his blond head. "The question is: what?"

"Can you meet with the gang? Maybe I can get Karis to take us up to Chace's to talk it out."

"I get off work at five."

"Okay, meet at my place if we don't pick you up."

My next stop was Cherise's. She was duly impressed by what I'd learned and agreed to come over just before five o'clock. Now, I had to convince my sister to take us up to see Chace.

*   *   *

"You want to go upriver *when*?" Mom exclaimed. "Harley, you've been up there all summer. I've hardly seen you."

"But, Mom, everyone can get off at that time. If we went up now, Will couldn't go."

I hadn't expected Mom to be the one to complain; Karis had readily agreed to the plan.

Mom sighed. "And what about family time?"

"We can come here for dinner if you want. I could invite Chace and Will to spend the night."

I got a sidelong glare.

"Honest, Mom." Karis pulled her hair into a ponytail. "I don't mind. I can bring them back for a late dinner. The guests would be all on their own by then anyway."

"Oh, all right. I'll expect you here by six-thirty, then. Cherise can stay for dinner and head home around nine."

"Thanks, Mom; you're the best!"

Mom grinned wearily. "I love you, too."

*   *   *

By five-thirty, we were all seated around the barn floor with Steria off to one side. She'd grown since I'd last seen her, and was now taller than any of us. She had to duck to go through the door that led to the room with the refrigerator, and her ribs brushed the frame.

After I'd told everyone about my dream, what I'd found out about the professor, and the conversation I'd overheard, there was a heavy pause. Then I asked, "What are we going to do?"

"Steria just needs to stay closer to home." Chace pushed up his glasses.

"That's not going to solve things. She needs to range that far to stay fed." Karis shook her head.

I looked around at our group of friends. Just a few months ago we were just three guys who liked to hang out together. Now we were all buddies, the girls included. It'd all happened because of a dragon.

Cherise leaned forward, her dark eyes intent. "I think the key was in Harley's dream." We all looked at her as if she was crazy. "The professor told Harley what to do. Like I said before, Steria needs a place away from people where she can be herself. We need to find a spot where she can relax and live on her own."

"I've already asked Mr. Behr to look. He hasn't come up with any suggestions yet."

"Even if he did, where would it be?" I could hear the bitterness in Chace's voice. He'd been the one to protect and care for Steria from the beginning. He had the most at stake if we shipped her off somewhere.

No one had an answer to his question. Since we'd told Mom we'd be home for dinner, we headed out, somber and discouraged. What to do when there was nothing that *could* be done? We all knew we couldn't hide her forever. Either we would find an answer or she'd be taken from us, one way or another. As I walked out to the car, Steria came alongside me.

Why must I not eat the lambs? she asked with a bowed head.

I stared at her. How to explain *that*?

"Steria," Will said, "the animals around here belong to people. They raise them for food and money. When you eat them, you're stealing."

And stealing is wrong?

I nodded. "It's taking what isn't yours. It'd be like the professor taking you from us."

He cannot do that. Smoke drifted from her nostrils.

I wanted to believe her, but couldn't.

"Stay here, Steria," Chace said. "And stay out of trouble."

She bowed her head, the pitiful motion reminding me of a puppy tucking its tail between its legs. I couldn't stand it, so I turned and left.

*   *   *

Dinner was fun. We all chatted with Mom and Dad, then Dad took his camera and did a silly photo shoot afterward. We made funny faces and took some group shots, and even Karis and Cherise joined in on the fun.

As soon as Cherise and Will left, I pulled out my phone and dialed. Standing on the front porch, I watched the sun set, the first stars already poking their heads out on the opposite horizon.

"Hi, Mr. Behr. Have you had any luck in finding a place for Steria?" I explained about what had happened that afternoon.

"Let me check back with my friend. I don't know what I'll find, but Cherise is right. We have to do something. If we don't, I have no choice but to hand her over to Professor Raleigh. I don't like the thought any more than you do, but I can't let her ruin the livestock up the river. Those men deserve to have their livelihood just as much as Steria deserves a safe place to live."

I had to agree. The facts were unavoidable. If it was a coyote or a cougar attacking the sheep, we'd all say to get the beast. Just because we knew the creature who was killing the livestock didn't mean we had the right to let her continue to do so.

I hung up with a feeling of defeat, not knowing whether things could be resolved. What would happen if we couldn't find somewhere for Steria to go? Images of a hunting party going after our dragon chased me all the way to sleep that night, leaving me heartsick and afraid.

CHAPTER 19: AN EXPLANATION OF SORTS

THE NEXT DAY, I was happily playing on the PS3 upstairs when Mom called.

"Harley." Something in her voice told me this wasn't good. "Please come down. Someone's here to see you."

I walked down the stairs slowly, afraid of who or what I'd find. Mom stood ashen-faced by the front door.

"Come on in here, Harley," she said in the same tone that she would use when she'd received a bad report card.

I followed her into the guest parlor and then froze in my tracks. Professor Raleigh stood in the sunlight streaming through the large bay windows. His suit jacket and tie stood out like the first rhododendron flowers in spring.

"Thank you, Mrs. Meagher. If you will excuse us."

Mom looked between the two of us. "And why can't I stay?"

He shook his head. "I am truly sorry, ma'am, but as I explained earlier, this is a matter of national security. I do not have the clearance to involve you. Unfortunately, your son and his friends stumbled upon the situation, and now I need to investigate what they know. If you would be so kind as to give us some privacy, I would greatly appreciate it. I really would."

Mom nodded and closed the French doors behind her, but I could tell she didn't like it one bit. In the seven years we'd lived here, I'd never seen those doors closed. Even seeing Mom standing on the other side of them and knowing she wouldn't leave didn't help me any. My stomach tightened into a knot as the professor reached into his pocket and pulled out his wallet. He opened it with a fluid, practiced motion, revealing a badge with the seal of the NSA.

"Go ahead and have a seat if you want, Harley," he instructed.

I nodded my head and took a wingback chair near the window. Mom and Dad's training made me indicate a seat for him. He sat on the edge of it. I didn't notice any evil grin or anything causing me to want to shrink away from him. Instead, he seemed honestly concerned for me.

"Harley, do you know why I am here?" He waited for my reply. When I didn't answer, he continued. "I really blame myself for this whole mess."

I glanced up at him in amazement. He gave a small, rueful smile and nodded.

"If I hadn't gotten sloppy and asked you and your friend to help look for the thundereggs, the scenario would be totally different, and we wouldn't have a national security risk in this little town." He paused and looked down at his hands. A car passed by on the highway. "Let me back up and give you some history, or, better stated, background information. You see, our world exists in its own time and place, but it isn't the only world in existence. There are other parallel universes. One of which holds all the creatures of fantasy, myth, and legend. These creatures live their lives completely unaware of our existence, and for the most part, we live believing they are just characters in story books. However, every so often, a hole develops that enables a mythical creature to travel to our world. No one really knows why; it just happens. I do not know if it goes both ways—so far, we haven't heard of anyone going to their realm. A special division of the NSA was created to respond to such challenges, a division of which I am part. It is a secret section that is never supposed to be talked about or known. You and your friends have changed that."

He looked directly into my eyes as he leaned forward with his elbows on his knees. I didn't know if I should be honored or afraid for what we'd done. He took a deep breath and continued.

"My supervisors believe you have shown yourselves worthy of keeping secrets, and that I can explain all of this to you. Back in April, when I first came to Myrtle Beach, our monitors had discovered another flicker in the space-time continuum, leading us to believe that a mythical creature would again enter our world. I came looking for that being. As I soon discovered, it was easier to find on the monitor than in real life. I believe you and your friends stumbled upon it and, for some unknown reason, decided to keep and protect this dangerous creature. You are harboring it up Myrtle River where it is attacking livestock and making a mess of its habitat. My supervisors and I are giving you an opportunity to make things right. We have a safe place where we protect all of these mythical beings. No one needs to know they exist, and they are no longer a threat to society. I am asking you to help me transport your creature to its new home."

He sat back and waited for my reply. I stared at him. Just yesterday, I was wondering where we could put Steria so she could be safe and would keep her home safe. I had no idea the professor would be the one to bring the answer. Despite his calm and quiet demeanor, I was still nervous. Again, the scenes of all the science fiction movies I'd seen filtered through my head. Too many times the government characters were the enemies.

"I wish I could help you, Professor."

"But?"

I shrugged.

"Harley, we already know the dragon is on Mr. Martin's ranch. I do not know if he is involved in the whole thing or not, but in any case you will not be able to keep it hidden for much longer. Word is spreading that the lamb kills are not the usual native predators. Someone just may learn the truth. When they do, there will be chaos."

I looked him straight in his brown eyes. "You can't be the one to tell them, or they will know all about your secret division. I think you're bluffing. You want me to tell you all I know and give you what you want, but I have no reason to trust you. You just want to get your hands on the dragon and do experiments on it."

He stared me down, but I didn't flinch. I would protect Steria. If Mr. Behr said to turn her over to the professor, then I would, but not until then.

The tall grass in the vacant lot next door waved in the breeze, catching my eye. I looked out at the beautiful day and wondered why I hadn't decided to ride my bike around town. I had a fleeting thought that maybe I could've avoided this encounter, but of course, I realized Professor Raleigh would've been waiting for me when I arrived home.

"Harley, if you change your mind, here is my card. Talk it over with your friends. Maybe one of them will be willing to talk to me."

He handed me his card. I took it, but wished I could lose it. He stood, which in rules of hospitality freed me to move as well, but I stayed in my seat looking at his card.

Professor Winston Patterson Raleigh, Ph.D. Biology
National Security Agency
Washington, DC
202-352-5595

I looked up when I heard the French doors open.

"Remember, Harley, you can call me at any time, day or night. If you wait too long, though, I won't be able to help. Others will step in..." he looked regretful, "and take *care* of the problem."

Mom opened the front door for him, and he walked out. I sat frozen in place. What should I do? What *could* I do? I stood up and did the one thing I could think of at that moment: I walked up to Karis's room and knocked.

The expression on her face when she opened the door said I'd disturbed her, but it quickly changed as she saw my face.

"What's up, Harley? You look like you've seen a ghost."

"Can I come in? I don't want Mom and Dad to hear."

*   *   *

Karis sat on her bed, her legs curled up to her chin, absently fiddling with a hair tie around her wrist. Her blonde hair flowed freely around her face and hung down around her shoulders. She flicked it off to the side.

"You mean he really *is* with the NSA, and he wants Steria?"

I nodded as I sat on the floor. Needing something for my hands to do, I picked at her throw rug, creating a pile of lint and dirt.

"What should we do?" she asked.

I shrugged. "That's why I came and talked with you. I don't know. When he was sitting there talking to me, a part of me wanted to do exactly as he said and turn her over, but the other part still said to protect her. I don't know how honest he's being about wanting to keep her from harm. He wants to protect the community, but I don't know about protecting her."

Karis nodded. "Let's let the others know, and then decide what we're going to do. We can also give Mr. Behr some time to figure things out."

*   *   *

We didn't get a chance to get together with the rest of the gang until the next evening. Will had worked at the crab shack all day, and Cherise had gone into town with her folks. When we finally gathered in the barn, I looked around, studying my friends. I wondered what'd happen if Professor Raleigh did talk with them. Would they give Steria up? Would Will give in for the money again? I couldn't say what they'd do.

"What's so important?" Chace leaned back against the wall.

I told them. When I was done, they wanted to see proof, so I handed the business card around. After everyone looked it over, Will spoke up.

"Harley, I know I got us into this mess. I really am sorry. I didn't think through everything. I just was tired of hearing Mom and Dad gripe about finances. No matter what the professor promises me, I won't betray Steria or you guys. Besides, I know she won't hurt us."

"Thanks, Will." I met his gaze. "I really don't blame you. I guess if Mom and Dad always fought over money, I'd have done the same thing."

His sincere blue eyes met mine. They spoke volumes, and I could almost see a weight lifted off his shoulders.

"That still doesn't answer the question of 'what do we do'," Cherise said. "If we keep her here, she'll keep killing livestock—probably more and more as she grows—and someone else will come after her. I heard in the market the other day that the ranchers are ready to call in the county trapper. Even if he can't catch her, he'll probably see her."

"She'd be a pretty big trophy to hang on someone's wall," Chace admitted.

"Let's give Mr. Behr a few more days to come up with an answer. In the meantime, we can all start looking at maps and see if there's anywhere we can send her." I suggested. "There's the Coast Range or the Cascades. A lot of that area is uninhabited. We might be able to have her fly there."

You all forget something. Steria stirred from her spot to look up at us. *I will not be captured. I will fight before that happens.*

"That's the problem, Steria." Karis ran a hand through her blonde hair. "If you fight, then people'll come after you. You'll hurt our friends and neighbors."

Then they should not try to attack me.

I shook my head. "Don't you see? You're destroying their livelihood, eating their food. They're going to come after you."

No matter how much we tried to convince her otherwise, Steria could not understand. I wondered what it was like where she came from. There was no way to know. Somehow, we had to think of something to protect Steria *and* our town.

CHAPTER 20: A MORNING RUN

ABOUT A WEEK went by. Professor Raleigh did approach Chace and his dad, but since Mr. Martin had never seen Steria and only seen the professor when he came by looking for lizards, he didn't give much credit to his story about national security. Will avoided the professor by working at the crab shack, where he kept busy out on the boats crabbing. Cherise hadn't been around us when the whole thing started, so she avoided being pestered by the professor.

I spent my afternoons riding around town. I'd eat at the market just to hear the local gossip. I heard all kinds of complaints about the unseasonably hot and dry summer we were having. All logging, road building, and even lawn mowing had pretty much shut down. Cranberry growers worried about having enough water for harvest come October. I'd never seen an Extremely High fire hazard warning before this summer, but it had been sitting there since the third week of July with no sign of going down. Smoke hazed the skies from fires inland, but none had reached us.

After eating my lunch one day, I took off on my bike. There wasn't anywhere in particular I was going; I just wandered around town. After a while I headed to the beach. Leaning my bike against the public restroom, I strolled down to the river's edge. I remembered the day when we'd found Steria and wondered what my summer would've been like without her. I wouldn't be going into the ninth grade with my senior sister as a friend and confidante, and I even doubted that Cherise would be considered one of my closest friends. I marveled at how much things could change from one small event.

A brownish shadow crossed the sand and turned the lighting an odd reddish-brown color. I looked up to see thick, billowing smoke.

This wasn't the far off smoke—it was too dense for that, signaling a fire much closer to us. I wondered if I needed to be concerned. The north wind wasn't blowing like it usually did in the summer. My phone rang in my pocket.

"Hello?"

"Harley, it's Mom. Where are you?" Her voice sounded panicked.

"I'm at the beach; why?"

"There's a fire up Myrtle River. It's spreading down toward town. They're talking about evacuating just to be on the safe side."

Evacuating?

"Harley?"

"I'm here, Mom."

"The people are going crazy. They say a dragon started the fire. Can you believe that?"

I could believe there was a dragon, but I couldn't believe she'd purposely start a fire. Besides, there was no way I could tell Mom that.

"A dragon?"

"Harley, please come home. We want the family to stay together, just in case we do need to leave."

I thought about it. I wanted to be with Steria and make sure she was safe. I wanted to know what'd caused the fire in the first place. I had no good answers. What could I do?

"Harley?"
"Yeah, Mom?"

"Never mind. Stay at the water. I'll try to make it to you."

"Mom, what if we meet at Grandma and Grandpa's across the river? It'll take me some time to get there, though."

"I don't know, Harley." There was silence and then a scream. I pulled the phone away from my ear.

"Mom? Mom!"

The call had been disconnected. I searched the sky toward my house. I was torn between searching for Steria and searching for my mom. My problem was that I didn't know if she was at home or not. She'd called from her cell and could be anywhere. My gaze turned east, toward home. What I saw made up my mind. Among the smoke, I caught a glimpse of purplish-red flames. I ran for my bike and turned upriver.

The road only went so far. I had to get onto the highway and backtrack to the river road. I knew it was crazy and even suicidal to be biking up Myrtle River Road, but there was nothing else I could do. I *had* to get to Steria. I pedaled determinedly, keeping my eyes pasted on the road in front of me, looking for any emergency vehicles heading back toward town and keeping my ears attuned to anything coming upriver.

About a quarter of a mile up, I came to the bridge, where I pulled over to let the volunteer fire department race by. In the meantime, I searched again for what I'd seen. The valley walls crowded in, making it impossible to see any real distance. The thick brown smoke also choked out any sight. My mind raced, wondering what to do.

In desperation, I called out, "Steria!" My voice hung in the air like dead weight, not going anywhere. However, I felt a flicker of her sense. I tried again.

Do not come any closer, Harley, her voice commanded. It filled my mind as if she'd just spoken right beside me.

"Steria, you must stop. Run, hide. Stop breathing fire! No more fires. Please!"

That is what Chace told me as well. I will try to go away, but where? I thought. Where could she go? Then it dawned on me.

"Steria, remember when we went on the river trip with our school? Go there. Come back tomorrow, but check to see if it's safe first."

I felt her hesitation. *But what about all of you?*

"We'll be fine. You just have to leave. Let us deal with this. If you're safe, we'll be fine."

Suddenly, her presence shifted, and soon it disappeared entirely. I felt empty. We were in deep trouble. I debated calling Professor Raleigh, but decided against it. Maybe Mr. Behr could help. I turned my bike around and headed to Grandma and Grandpa's.

*   *   *

Karis was already there, and she wrapped me up in a tight hug that I was too scared to mind very much. Dad left work and paced Grandpa's garage until Mom pulled into the driveway. Then we all gathered in front of the radio to listen for an evacuation order. But instead, a few hours later we got the all clear. No buildings lost. A hundred acres or so of forest gone, but no human casualties. We breathed a collective sigh of relief and Mom cried a little and hung onto Dad, though she hadn't done that while we waited.

Mom had been relieved to find me, but she rambled about having seen a dragon when she was on the phone with me. Apparently that's why she'd screamed, and then the phone had gone dead when she dropped it. It was now in pieces on the kitchen table, and Dad was patiently trying to reassemble it. I tried to calm Mom, but not much was going to reassure her, especially with the rumors that a dragon had started the wildfire. Dad didn't have much better luck. Eventually he shook his head and said quietly to me, "She'll be more rational about it tomorrow." I felt a little guilty for letting him think Mom was hysterical, but what else could I do?

Mr. Behr called later to check in, and he did have some good news. I found out that he had a friend who owned an island in the Pacific off the coast of Oregon. It didn't have any human inhabitants, and it had a good ecosystem that could probably handle the addition of a dragon. Besides the local animals, Steria could also catch fish. We just had to get her there.

I met with Will, Cherise, and Karis the next morning. The flames had been contained the night before, and, at least officially, no one knew how it had been started. All of us breathed a sigh of relief. Steria confessed that she had accidentally started the fire while she was hunting. I told them what Mr. Behr had found.

"We need a way to get Steria out to the island. I don't know how far she can fly. Mr. Behr said it was almost outside of the US boundary waters and further south of here."

"The US boundary waters are fourteen miles out, and if it's southerly, too, it's even farther for her," Will said. "I don't know if she can fly that far without stopping."

"Most birds can fly that." I rested my chin on my hands. "But I don't know if Steria is up to that yet. According to Chace, she's still landing pretty frequently on longer jaunts."

"That means we need a boat." Cherise looked up at Will. "Where can we find one big enough for a dragon?"

"A dragon and us." Karis twirled her hair around her finger. "We need to all be able to go, and Mr. Behr will have to guide us there."

I sighed. This was looking less and less likely to actually work.

"I can get a boat." Will's shy voice was suddenly confident. "Carl said I can use his anytime I needed it."

I raised an eyebrow. "Is it big enough for all of us?"

He nodded. "Yep. When do we want to try to do this?"

"Let me call Mr. Behr," I said.

Mr. Behr suggested we try to move her the next day. That'd give Will time to secure the boat, Chace to find Steria, and us to get her to the docks.

*   *   *

That night, my nightmare returned. I was running from the professor, Steria ahead of me. Only this time, she billowed fire around her. Her flames licked up the webbing Professor Raleigh used, and its flaming bits started small fires everywhere they landed. I tried to put them out before anyone could see them and come for Steria, but no matter what I did, the fires grew, and the Professor walked right through them, coming for me and shooting his web. When I awoke, I was panting. My covers were on the floor, and I could barely breathe. I snatched my inhaler from the nightstand and took a deep draught.

As my breathing stabilized, I wondered if the nightmare would go away once Steria was on the island. I hoped so. I knew my asthma would stay with me, but hopefully it would calm down. Usually I didn't have this many attacks in a month. I laid back down and tried to go to sleep, but my mind was racing as heavily as my heart.

What would tomorrow bring? Had Chace found Steria? What if Will couldn't get the boat for some reason? What was the island like? Then there were all the questions swarming in my head about the town's reaction to a dragon among them. I tossed and turned. Nothing helped. When the first morning light came through my window, I got up.

No one else was awake yet, but I went ahead and fixed myself some breakfast. After putting my dishes in the dishwasher, I wandered outside. The day was already too warm. I tried to expend my excess energy by jogging in place. It didn't work. I sighed and rubbed my eyes.

A distant sound, something between a squawk and a roar, caught my attention. I turned in the direction of the sound, but the mountains blocked any view. With nothing better to do, I jogged toward Hubbard Mountain Road. This early in the morning, the only thing I needed to worry about was meeting a log truck coming down the mountain, but since logging had been suspended, I figured it should be safe.

The road wound upward sharply at first, and my breathing became heavier. Finally, the road straightened out a bit. I paused, taking in deep gulps of air and looking out toward the western horizon. The ocean spread out below me in varying shades of blues and greens. Clouds scuttled across the sky, creating darker patches of color on the water beneath. From this vantage point, I could see miles to the north, south, and west, but not far to the east. The mountain still rose behind me.

The sound came again, perhaps from near the river? I turned toward the south and east. Down in the valley lay the Myrtle River, wending its way eastward. If the river ran straight, I'd be able to see up it all the way to Chace's house, but since it twisted and curved as it cut its way through the mountains and on down to the beach, I could only see a mile or two along its length. What I saw spurred my feet into another jog.

Steria flew down the river, banking and coming more toward Hubbard Mountain. Behind her trailed a small plane! I picked up my pace so she'd intersect with me. At the same time, my mind raced, trying to come up with a plan. I was on Hubbard Mountain, which meant Camp Pinewood was only a couple of miles further up. Thanks to track and cross-country I was pretty confident that I could go two more miles, even if it had been a few months since I had run. I settled into a pace that would eat up the distance without exhausting me.

Steria! I thought, *Come to me. I'll take you to safety.*

I saw her body shift as she sped up. The plane was too small to keep up with Steria's strong wings for a short distance, but it was gaining on her. I was glad that Hubbard Mountain jutted up and then dropped away to the north. I motioned for Steria to come quicker. She picked up some speed, but I could tell she was approaching the limits of her endurance. With a swoop, she turned toward me, gliding through the air close to the ground. I pointed for her to go up the road and into the forest and ran after her.

As soon as we were behind the trees, I had her land out of sight of the road until the plane passed. The trees were too dense for the plane to fly through, but it circled several times. Not until it headed off north did I start moving again. I jogged up the road and had Steria follow me. At the same time, I texted Karis. I needed to let her know what was happening and where I was. Mom and Dad would have a fit if they woke up and couldn't find me.

The camp was another mile up from where the forest gathered in over the road. I settled down into my cross-country mode, designed to conserve energy and still place in a meet. The evergreens stretched from one side of the road to the other. Cones and needles littered the ditches. The road had narrowed so much that Steria couldn't really fly. She walked-hopped alongside me, her stride easily keeping pace with mine.

In no time at all, the road turned and headed downward, twisting and turning all the way. Just as it wound back up another slope, I saw my destination on my right. The trees thinned to admit a small chapel on the hill; lower down they parted to allow a basketball court and a dining room. Further down, cabins sat in two lines under tall, stately conifers. During camp season, the place was filled to overflowing with kids and adults running around playing carpet pool and basketball. It seemed eerily quiet. Today, however, I was thankful there wasn't a camp in session.

"Come on, Steria," I said into the sounds of wind sighing through the firs and birds chirping. "We're going to stay here for now. Then later we can go to the dock."

My phone chirped. I looked down, surprised to see that I still had reception, and found that Karis had sent me a text.

Meeting Mr. Behr at the dock at 10:00. Will will have the boat ready. I'll get Chace and Cherise there.

I looked at the time and saw that I still had two and a half hours to kill. I started ambling down the driveway to the dining room, but at the sound of a plane, I thought better of our location and headed to the cabins under the trees. The plane passed over without incident, and I breathed a sigh of relief. Steria curled up beside me and lay down to wait.

*   *   *

Sometime during the morning, I dozed off. When I awoke, my mouth was protesting the fact that I'd run without drinking anything afterward. I stretched and pulled out my phone. It was almost time to head back down the hill and try to meet up with the others.

"Let's get moving, Steria. I'll get a drink at the water fountain, and then we'll head back down to the river."

The water was refreshing and helped wake me up. Wiping my face with it as well, I looked up the driveway and signaled to Steria.

We'd made it just about to the tree line when Steria stretched her wings and resumed her blend of a hop and a flight. It was slightly humorous. She paused in mid-stride and turned to me.

I am funny? she asked.

I nodded.

I am not *funny,* she stated, her dignity clearly affronted.

"Oh come on, Steria. You look funny."

Suddenly, her expression changed. A growl seemed to rumble in her throat.

"What's wrong, Steria?"

I turned to look where she was staring and froze at what I saw. On the road behind us walked a man. From the silhouette I could tell he held a device in his hand. My mind flashed back to the nightmare I'd had. Even though it was just a shadow against the rising sun, I knew it was the same weapon Professor Raleigh pointed at me in the dream.

"Run, Steria, run!" I called frantically. "I'm right behind you."

I took off, careful to not trip on the downhill road. I hoped beyond hope that everyone would be at the dock. My mind took a distracted moment to wonder what people would think seeing a dragon flying over the town, and after the fire incident, I was sure it wouldn't go unnoticed. I knew I'd have a lot to explain to my neighbors *and* my parents.

I pushed that thought aside as I heard Professor Raleigh call out, "Harley, stop!"

My feet moved faster. I hoped to stay ahead of the professor. If he fit anywhere into the academic stereotype, he shouldn't be in shape to run downhill for another mile. I'd learned to never look over my shoulder. I'd tried it once or twice and each time it had ended in me plastering my face with gravel, and I didn't have time for such mistakes. Too much depended on this race. Instead, I buckled down and ran.

Steria flew ahead of me, and even with all the stress, I was able to admire her grace in flight. As I came into town, I was glad to see that there weren't many people outside. However, as I passed the market, someone waved, then gasped. I kept running, disregarding the sounds of fright behind me, and turned down Myrtle River Road toward the docks.

My breath was getting labored enough to be painful by the time I rounded the crab shack. I only had about a block left, and I could see where Steria had landed and was waiting for me. Despite the pounding in my chest and the lack of breath, I forced myself to continue. Just off the dock a boat bobbed in the water, Chace and Karis looking toward me from the lower deck. The fear on my sister's face caused me to pause and glance over my shoulder, despite every thought that I shouldn't. What I saw made my breath catch against my chest.

No! my mind screamed as my lungs tightened. Behind me, Professor Raleigh raised his weapon. A boom sounded. I ducked and ran, although not as fast as I had before. A spray of white film landed on the walkway ahead of me. My lungs wouldn't let my legs run any faster; besides my muscles were already killing me. I had no breath to yell a warning to Steria. Another explosion echoed in my ears. The white web wrapped itself around Steria's neck. She shook her head, turned, and spewed fire. The heat rushed into my face. I couldn't stop; so, I plowed right through it, thankful to find that it dissipated as quickly as it had come.

"Harley!" Karis screamed. "Come on!"

I didn't bother to answer. I just pelted toward the dock. Chace turned and helped Steria find a place on the boat. Another pop sounded, and it felt as if a giant hand pushed me the last few feet to the edge of the pier, but I tripped on a cleat and lost my balance. If it hadn't been for Karis, I would have fallen into the river. My sister grabbed me by my shirt and pulled me physically up onto the boat.

"Go, Will!" she hollered.

The sudden acceleration threw me backwards even as I struggled to catch my breath, driving me away from Karis' pull. I plopped unceremoniously onto my backside, my lungs spasming and refusing to fill while the surf jounced the boat, exacerbating the breathless sensation that clawed at my chest. The vessel veered away from the dock, allowing me to take in the scene behind me. People had congregated around Professor Raleigh, probably drawn from the shops and restaurant by the sound of the web gun. The professor stood, his weapon no longer in sight, with a look of frustration and defeat on his face.

I had no breath to shout a victory cry. Instead, I groped in my pocket for my inhaler and sucked down the life-giving drug. This time, I'd literally run a race in the midst of what felt like trying to breathe through a straw. I didn't suggest it to anyone. However, I knew that my nightmare wouldn't plague me anymore. I'd played it out, and I'd triumphed. I watched the shoreline recede until Professor Raleigh was an indistinct speck on the dock, then turned and faced the open ocean. We had a dragon to deliver to her new home.

CHAPTER 21: A BOAT RIDE

I DIDN'T WANT to think of what it was going to be like when we returned to our once sleepy little town, but for now, we were safe.

"Ugh, what is this stuff?" Chace picked at the white film on my shoulder.

I shrugged. "I'm not sure. I just know that, in my nightmares, it created a web."

Chace looked at me as if I'd grown horns.

"You don't want to know. Anyway, it came from the professor's weapon. He shot it at me and Steria."

"I saw something on her but didn't know what it was. It doesn't want to come off of her, either."

I nodded. "I think it's designed to act as a rope or net to trap something. It shouldn't cause us any harm now, though, I think."

"Well, let's get you both as cleaned up as best we can." Karis reached a hand out to help steady me against the roll of the boat, then headed toward the bow of the craft, followed by Chace and Steria.

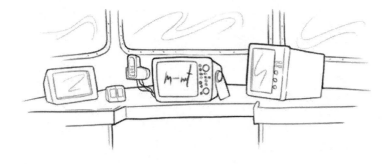

I trailed behind them and looked around. The stern was an open, flat area that would've been used to carry a haul of fish or crab pots, depending on the client. Stretching overhead were two long poles that could be lowered to drag nets on either side of the boat.

Suddenly, I was brought up short as I ran into Steria. She'd stopped outside a door.

"What's wrong, Steria?"

The opening is too small. I cannot enter.

I looked up and realized she was right. We'd always had her trail along with us at the barn and had gotten accustomed to the scale of the doorways there. Here, they were made only for people, not equipment or animals.

I bent around her. "Karis, you'll have to bring the water outside. Steria can't fit in there."

Chace stuck his head back out. At the same time, I heard footsteps above us and looked up to see Cherise descending the ladder to the left of the smokestack.

Above her, Mr. Behr looked down over the railing. "How's everything?"

I nodded. "She doesn't fit in human doors anymore."

"Of course she can't," Cherise said. "Why'd you want her inside when we have this wide-open deck for her?"

Karis came around Chace carrying a bucket and a rag. "I wanted to clean this stuff off them. Harley can go on in and clean up his shirt, but Steria has this gunk all over her neck."

"Can I help?" Cherise asked.

Karis nodded. "I could use all the help I can get." She raised her voice. "Mr. Behr, we need your help to get this stuff off of Steria. Can you come down?"

Mr. Behr laughed. "What did she get into this time?"

"It's not something she got into." I backed away to see him better. "Professor Raleigh shot her and me with some kind of gun that sent out a sticky webbing of some kind. It hit me on the back, but it got Steria on her neck."

I slipped off my shirt and walked around my sister into the small room below deck. Will sat at the helm, gazing not only at the river's mouth and the ocean beyond, but at the various gadgets and two panels showing a map, radar, and what I assumed must be a topographical map of the river bed going by beneath us. I grabbed the back of a bench seat connected to a table beside me as a wave pushed me off balance.

"You'll get used to it eventually." Will glanced to me and then back out the front windows.

I steadied myself using the counter on my right and stepped past a miniature fridge with a microwave tied down to its top. I plugged up the tiny sink and grabbed a bottle of water from the counter above me. As it filled, I plunged my shirt into the basin and began rubbing it vigorously, but the sticky mass was stubborn, and even adding soap didn't help. Shaking my head in frustration, I wrung out the shirt and pulled it back on while I climbed the steps back to the deck, shivering in the cool breeze. The others stood scrubbing at Steria's neck. She stood glaring at them.

Enough! A growl punctuated her words. *It is not coming off. It is not harming me; let it be.*

Mr. Behr was the first to step away. The others soon followed suit and dropped their rags into the bucket.

"I didn't have much luck either." I turned to show them my wet shirt.

"Well, what do we do now?" Chace dried his hands on his Carharts.

"I'm hungry. Breakfast was too many hours ago." My stomach rumbled. "Do we have anything?"

Karis nodded. "You're in luck, Harley. Mom packed us a lunch. Let's go share it with Will. Steria, you can be right outside."

Inside, Karis slid a board out from the wall, which covered the sink to create a counter. We all climbed down the steps behind her, and Chase and Cherise slid into the far seat at the table. I took the spot across from them.

My eyes went to Will at the helm. This was not the friend I knew from school. He was confident and poised as he maneuvered the boat through the swells.

"Mr. Behr, can you take a look at that map and tell me where exactly we're going?" he asked. "Once we're further out to sea, I can stop and get my bearings."

"Sure," Mr. Behr replied, and he stepped up to the panel on Will's right.

Our teacher pulled a piece of paper out of his pocket and unfolded it, displaying some neatly handwritten numbers. At first, I thought it was some complicated math problem. "Do you want me to put it into the GPS?" he asked.

Karis handed me a sandwich, breaking my concentration on Mr. Behr. I nodded my thanks.

"Is this what you've been doing since the Fourth?" I asked Will around a bite of Mom's ham sandwich.

He nodded, then pointed. "See over there? That change in the water color? That's where I'd take fishermen to get their catch. Closer to shore's where we do crabbing, or in the river itself."

I stood amazed. My friend who barely spoke at school and rarely had answers on his tests seemed to know all about fishing on the ocean. He turned and looked back toward shore. The few boats we could see didn't seem to be following us. Will flipped a switch, and the gentle rumble in the deck below our feet stopped. He looked around, flipped another switch, and then turned in his chair and stood. A grin spread across his face, realizing we'd made it safe so far.

"Where's Steria?"

We pointed to the door, but at the same time heard her voice. *I am safe. Thank you for guiding this water creature.*

"It's the least I could do after telling the professor about you in the first place. Now, let me see where we're headed…"

He looked at Mr. Behr's coordinates, and his eyes grew large.

"What's wrong, Will?" Cherise crumpled her napkin into a ball.

"That's a ways out there. We may have to contact your folks, not to mention Carl—I won't be getting this boat back to him any time soon. I didn't think it was *that* far away."

I looked to Karis with raised eyebrows.

"How far do we have to go?" Chace fell against Cherise as a wave rocked the boat sideways.

"We'll be out here for approximately twenty-four hours. That's twelve to our destination and twelve back. I can only get this trawler to go so fast; some favorable conditions will give us a few more knots, but it won't make a big difference."

Even Cherise's normally unflappable demeanor seemed shaken. "Twelve hours before we even get there?"

Will nodded. "You might as well call home and let your parents all know."

"I'll call them." Mr. Behr pulled out his cell phone and held several brief conversations. They mostly consisted of the same answers in response to obviously anxious parents. There was one more thing I had to look forward to—explaining to Mom why I'd run off without so much as telling her

When our teacher hung up, his face was grim. "Well, guys, we have our work cut out for us. The people of Myrtle Beach are pretty riled up. The professor has personally been to the Meaghers', Martins', and the crab shack. He's demanding that we turn around right this instant as a matter of national security. The adults have all told him that the best interest of the town is to keep the dragon as far away as possible. I've assured them that's exactly what we're doing, so at this point they don't care who takes Steria as long as she leaves town. I get the feeling they'd rather keep their heads down and let things play out as they may. They've told the professor that he can follow us if he wants to, but they're not involved."

* * *

Land was a mere speck on the horizon at our bow. I was grateful for the GPS. I wondered how in the world those old sailors plotted their courses by the stars. I wouldn't want to have to try it, that's for sure. The sun was still high in the sky, but it was on the downward side of its daily path. The sunset would be off our starboard bow when it came, and with the clear weather, it should be gorgeous. However, a somber mood had come over the passengers as we mulled over what Mr. Behr had relayed from home. If we didn't want anyone discovering where we'd left Steria, we'd have to leave her and never return to see her. I couldn't imagine that. I'd somehow assumed that since Will had access to a boat, we could just go see her any time we wanted to. Now, that didn't seem feasible without someone following us—either Professor Raleigh or someone else eager to see a dragon. I wondered how it was that he wasn't tracking us right now, then realized I had no assurance that he wasn't doing exactly that. The thought sent a shiver through me.

"You cold, Harley?" Cherise asked as we both sat up on the lookout.

I shook my head. "No, just thinking about Professor Raleigh."

"Him! Why bother? He's not worth thinking about."

"Unless he's trying to follow us."

In shock, she glanced back toward land. "You think he would?"

I shrugged. "I don't know. Maybe."

"What's wrong, you two?" Chace climbed the ladder and stood behind us. "You look like you've seen a ghost."

"Harley thinks the Professor's following us."

Chace also glanced over his shoulder. "Nah, we would've seen him by now."

"What if he's using some sort of satellite tracking device?" I grabbed the railing to keep from sliding into Cherise.

Both Chace and Cherise exchanged glances. We were silent as we thought of the possibilities.

"Well, we can't fight what we can't see." Chace spread his feet and leaned against the rail. "We might as well enjoy our time while we can. Will says we're going too fast to fish, but we can at least enjoy the sun and the waves."

We might not have been able to fish, but the speed of the trawler didn't interfere with Steria's tactics at all. To our delight, she loved leaping off the deck, soaring into the air, skimming the surface of the waves, and snatching fish out of the ocean.

"Look at her go!" Cherise called, as Steria dove from the sky like a jet that'd lost all power.

"Pull up, pull up!" I yelled, but Steria parted the waters head first.

To my surprise, she resurfaced and paddled over to the boat where she arched her neck to deposit her catch on the decking and watched it flop around. Then with a screech of metal, she used the side of the boat to launch herself back into the air.

"Crazy dragon." Karis shook her head. "Scare us half to death. Where'd she learn how to swim?"

A lake in the mountains kept me occupied while you were worried about Professor Raleigh.

The mention of the professor reminded me of the reason for our voyage. We were allowing Steria to be free, but it also meant good-bye for us.

CHAPTER 22: AN ISLAND PARADISE

A GORGEOUS SUNSET gave way to sparkling stars. Occasionally we saw other lights from ships on the horizon, but Will assured us they were not following, just out fishing. Will let the autopilot take over while we ate a late supper, then we all wandered off on our own. Mr. Behr stood at the prow. Cherise and Karis found a corner and sat chatting quietly. I could just make out their forms in the dark. Chace stretched out on a bench. Steria lay sprawled on the deck. I looked back toward shore and found only darkness.

My mind was still trying to grasp what had actually happened this morning and the gravity of what we were doing. Somehow, a very law-abiding eighth grade citizen had defied the NSA. My brain couldn't wrap itself around the fact. I had run through town, evading the law and scaring the people I had known my whole life half to death. A sparkle of amethyst color caught my eye, and I glanced over to see Steria looking directly at me.

Thank you, Harley, she said quietly. *I appreciate it.*

I shook my head. It was beyond reason. A creature I'd known for only a few months had completely turned my priorities upside down. How could this be? And yet, it felt right. I was destined to protect her.

"You're welcome. I just don't know what I'm going to do when I get home. I know I'll be grounded for life, and that'll just be the beginning."

Steria closed her eyes as if it was nothing to her. My thoughts continued to churn. This dragon, a creature that before April I would have said didn't exist, had permanently enmeshed herself in my heartstrings. Now, I couldn't imagine life without her. Out of the corner of my eye I caught the motion of Chace turning over. What must he be going through? He had nurtured her, fed her, and defended her. He had watched her grow from an egg to a small dragon. He had seen her learn to fly and spout fire. He also had seen the destruction her fire had caused. I sighed. I wanted to cry, but that wouldn't help matters now. In the glow of the signal lights, I watched our dragon breathe. And tried to come to terms with giving her away.

*　*　*

At some point, I must have fallen asleep. A yellow glow brought me back to wakefulness. The sun had popped over the horizon, reflecting off the ocean waves. The glare dimmed to a beautiful green as we sank into a trough, then returned in all its brilliance as we rode up the next wave. I stretched and rubbed my back. The metal decking was chilly and not the most comfortable bed. Across the deck, Steria's scales glowed almost with a life of their own. I couldn't believe I'd never noticed that before. They seemed to soak up the sun rays and then emit them in a rainbow of violet hues.

Curled up against her side was Chace. My thoughts of the night before came crashing in on me like the surf. How would Chace be able to say good-bye to her? The sorrow dogged my steps as I made my way to the wheelhouse.

Will sat in the captain's chair, the light making his blond hair glow.

"Morning," he greeted me.

"Morning."

"There's muffins in the cupboard there if you want some breakfast. We should be at the island in about a half hour."

"Were you awake all night?" I asked as I rummaged in the cupboard and found not only muffins, but also orange juice packets and some fruit.

"No, I shut down the boat and slept. I probably could have let it go on autopilot, but I wouldn't have trusted it once we were closer to shore." He pointed out the window. Sure enough, I could see the form of land. "It's a good thing, too. There's a reef quite a ways offshore. I'm not really sure how we're going to land, short of swimming."

I shivered. Swimming in the Pacific Ocean this far north was always tricky—and cold. There were undertows, and the current came directly from Alaska. Survival time for capsized boats was twenty minutes of unprotected exposure to the water. Will must have read my thoughts.

"I'm hoping Mr. Behr has some maps of the place. Maybe there'll be a dock we can tie up to."

I hoped so. This was going to be hard enough without adding swimming in unknown Pacific waters.

"I see we've arrived," Mr. Behr's voice greeted us. "Try to circle to the east; Jason said there should be a dock to tie up to somewhere on that side. Careful of the reef, though. After that, he said it should be easy enough."

Will nodded. "I saw the reef. Any idea where to enter?"

Mr. Behr shrugged. "Do you have any equipment that will see the bottom?"

"I thought about that, but it won't see far enough ahead. I'll have to trust my instincts and my eyes."

"I'll go let the others know," I said, and turned to leave.

The girls were stretching when I found them. Cherise bounded to her feet when I told her we were close. Karis, never a morning person, moved more slowly. When I reached Chace and Steria, I paused. He wouldn't want to hear that we had arrived. But I also knew that he wouldn't want to miss any of the remaining time he had with her. I woke him gently.

Why are you sad, Harley? Steria inquired as I roused my friend. *Is this not what you had planned?*

I nodded. "I guess, but I thought we could come and visit you whenever we wanted. Now we have to stay away, or else people will follow us or Professor Raleigh will find you."

"Thanks for the reminder, Harley," Chace said, pushing his glasses up on his face.

"Sorry," I mumbled. "She asked."

Chace shrugged awkwardly, and I could tell he was trying to avoid the subject. "What's up?"

"We're almost there—Steria could fly the distance we have left. Breakfast is in the wheelhouse. Will is going to have to avoid a reef to get near, but then there's a dock to tie up to."

"Well, let's see your new home, Steria." Chace stood and stretched, then adjusted the suspenders his mom had given him.

When he was ready, we headed back to the wheelhouse.

*   *   *

"Watch out!" Cherise called from the flybridge. "You're too far to the right."

Will adjusted his course while the rest of us held our breath. From where she stood, Cherise had a better view of the ocean and what lay in front of us, but everyone else was essentially blind in the glare of the water. After a few more adjustments, Cherise yelled down, "I think we're clear! I don't see any more rocks."

"And I think I see the dock, there off your starboard side," Mr. Behr directed.

Will nodded and made for the little pier. Within fifteen minutes, we had tied up and were standing on solid ground. It felt strange to not feel the movement beneath our feet—I kept stumbling as I tried to walk. I was surprised by how quickly I'd adjusted to the sway of the boat under me.

"Welcome to your new home, Steria," Mr. Behr said. "My friend, Jason, says this island is only used for conservation and study. He'll check in occasionally, but for the most part you'll have the place to yourself. As long as you promise to not eat everything in sight and be friendly to Jason, you'll be fine here."

Steria nodded solemnly. *Well, then, let us explore my new home.*

Mr. Behr and the girls headed toward the small cabin just up the hill from the dock, while Will stayed with the boat.

With stately grace, Steria leapt into the air, her wings iridescent in the morning light. I looked at Chace and shrugged. He grinned and began running, following behind her. I joined him. The ground sloped upward at a gentle angle. Dried grass crunched under our feet. As we rounded the hill, the grass disappeared and gave way to rock. It was the same crumbling stone that comprised the cliffs off the shore of Myrtle Beach. The wind had taken its toll and worn down the rocky surface, leaving flaking shale in place of the solid ground it once had been. The plateau stretched for about a mile and then disappeared from sight. Sea birds lifted off the rough crags, squawking as they went. These birds were in for a shock. Their home would have another occupant. In the air, Steria circled in great, gliding loops, bugling her joy and dashing through the salty spray that leapt from the breakers up the face of the cliffs. I looked over and saw Chace watching her, a bright smile on his face, hardly touched with any sadness.

On the west side of the rock shelf, it dropped in a sheer cliff to the ocean below. I backed away, not wanting to get too close to the precipitous edge. To the south, a more gradual slope met my gaze, fading into a meadow where cattle and deer were grazing. I stared, wondering how on earth deer got onto the island. Beyond the meadow, trees rose toward the sky. From my vantage point, they were like a blanket covering that side of the island.

I don't know how long I stood gazing out to sea before I heard voices shouting. Far up on the hilltop, figures waved. I raised my arms and waved back. One of the people—Mr. Behr, from the silhouette—came toward me. Steria sat in the middle of the clearing. I met Mr. Behr by Steria, who had stretched out and pointedly ignored us. Beside her lay Chace.

Mr. Behr looked at us with a sad, knowing smile. "We have a long trip ahead of us. We can take a few more moments, but let's at least start heading in the general direction of the dock."

Steria stirred, and I caught a feeling of remorse and fear. It wasn't my emotion, but I sensed it as fully as if it had been. Chace must have felt it, too, because he laid a hand on her flank. Some of the apprehension ebbed immediately as she leaned ever so slightly into the touch.

"Mr. Behr," Chace spoke up. "We need to give Steria time to adjust before we leave."

"I know, Chace, but we need to head back, as well. We can easily stay another twenty minutes or so, but let's head back to the cove. Will's waiting for us."

"Come on, Steria," I said.

She sat up and pushed off into the sky, where she circled the meadow once and then flew off in a straight line for the dock.

"She'll be fine, Chace," I said into the stillness.

He nodded, but it was stiff and pained. We walked in silence the rest of the way.

As we came down the path to the dock, I saw Steria perched on a rock. I nudged Chace and pointed to her. He nodded and adjusted his suspenders.

Will greeted us. "There you guys are! I didn't want to leave the boat. Carl will have my hide if anything happens to it."

"Not to mention not being able to get home, right?" I laughed. Chace seemed awfully quiet. "You okay?" I asked him in an undertone.

He shrugged and turned to watch Steria. The memories of the first week of summer ran through my mind. I remembered our surprise as we felt the tapping from her shell for the first time, laughter as she knocked Karis to the barn floor, and horror mixed with amazement as we saw her breathe fire for the first time. Will hopped out of the boat and walked over to us. We stood, silent and suddenly somber, staring at our dragon.

A hand on my shoulder startled me. Karis stood behind me with Cherise beside her. Our normally cheery friend stood with her face fixed in a tight-jawed fight against tears, her large brown eyes pools of emotion. I heard her voice in my memory saying, "It's a dragon, of course." I replayed the awe we all felt as we saw the egg hatch. I remembered Steria inquiring about Mr. Behr. I looked over my left shoulder to where he stood beside Karis. He, too, was far from his usual jolly self.

Steria stirred on her perch and began to preen her wings as if nothing was wrong. A lump formed in my throat. I didn't want to do what I knew was necessary. I could only imagine how Chace was feeling.

"Steria," Karis called, her voice thick. "Can you come here? I don't want to talk to you over this distance."

The dragon paused, looked my sister in the eyes, and then flew up into the air. She alighted a distance away, and Karis walked to where she landed. I watched as my sister hugged our dragon, and I saw Karis wipe her eyes as she turned and came back to the boat.

Mr. Behr waited until she had returned before he approached Steria. Cherise stood beside me now, Will on my other side Chace still faced out to sea.

"What now?" Will asked. "What do we do?"

"What we've always done," Cherise said. "If we were friends before Steria, we can still be friends when she's gone."

I wanted to believe her, but I wasn't too sure. I watched as Cherise traded places with Mr. Behr and threw her arms around Steria. The two stayed that way for a long while. When Cherise turned back toward us, I saw the sun glistening off tears streaming down her cheeks.

"Well, I suppose it's my turn," Will said. I heard the regret in his voice.

"Will," I stopped him from leaving. He turned to me. "It's okay. No one holds it against you."

He shook his head. "Harley, I was wrong to tell Professor Raleigh about Steria's egg. I didn't want to believe you guys. Mom and Dad are always arguing over money. I thought... I thought I could help, but..."

"I know, Will," I interrupted. "I didn't help by making you give me your backpack, but you've more than made up for it by piloting us out here."

"But if I hadn't told him, she might still be with us, and Chace..." he looked helplessly at our grieving friend.

"No," I told him firmly. "We'd have had to find a new place for her anyway. Who knows how big she's going to get? We couldn't hide her forever. And without you, Steria would be hiding from the professor and all of Myrtle Beach. Or worse, she'd be going to some NSA holding ground and we'd never know if she was okay."

He nodded. "Thanks, Harley. I needed that."

"No problem."

He smiled, and that's when I realized that Cherise was right. Steria hadn't been the reason for our friendship; she had only strengthened it.

The water lapped at the pilings beneath us. Chace hadn't moved from his place. I knew the turmoil inside him. I felt the pull to stay, but I was coming to grips with everything. Steria would be fine here without us. The run up on top of the hill had proven that to me. I could let her be here. The harder part was to leave and not come back. "Chace?" I called, pitching my voice just louder than the sound of the waves. He didn't move. "Chace?" I tried again.

"Harley, I can't do this." he said.

"I know," I agreed. "But it'll be okay. We'll be fine."

He shook his head. "I can't leave her. She'll be lonely here. She needs company. No animal here thinks and communicates like she does."

He paused to take a breath. I understood his feelings, but I didn't want him to miss out on saying goodbye, and we did need to go home soon.

"Chace, we'll be fine. And so will she."

He shook his head. "I can't. There's a nice cabin over there. You guys can bring me supplies. There's enough fish and game. I'll be fine here."

I didn't think he was serious until he looked at me. His eyes showed the hurt, but also determination.

"Chace, what about your dad?"

That seemed to stop him in his tracks. It was like I had put a pin in a balloon. He stood there staring at me. Then he turned and walked to Steria, and stood beside her with his hand on her shoulder. Everyone else had boarded, and they were looking back expectantly. I shook my head and followed my friend.

"Chace," I said when I reached him, but he held up a hand to stop me. I sighed and moved to Steria's other side.

"Hi, girl," I said.

Hello, Harley.

"Can you talk sense into Chace?" I asked her.

I heard her low rumble of a laugh, and I was forced to acknowledge that common sense had not had much of a role in our decision making since we found her egg. I giggled. She joined in, and even Chace added his laughter to ours. Soon it was a rolling sound, the three of us together in the face of our parting. But when it died down, I knew I still had to convince my friend to come home.

"Chace, I understand how you feel. You've been like a dad to Steria. You've fed her, watched over her, and taken care of her. Hey, you've even used the shotgun to scare Professor Raleigh away!"

Chace chuckled as he recalled that moment.

"See. I know what you're going through."

"No, Harley, you don't," he said. "You've never had to watch someone you love slip away from you. You've never had to tell them good-bye."

I swallowed and winced at the raw pain in his voice He continued. "When Mom died, I promised that if I ever loved someone, I'd never let them leave again."

The memories of our fifth grade year came back to me. I remembered the struggle as Mrs. Martin fought the cancer, only to succumb at home over spring break.

"When we found the egg," Chace said. "I knew I had no control over it. Steria wormed her way into my heart, and I knew I could never say good-bye to her."

"Oh, Chace," I sighed. "I'm sorry. I really am." I was at a loss for words. I thought of the day when I had gone to his house, back while his mom was still alive. Knowing her time was running out, she had pulled me aside.

"Harley, I know you are Chace's friend. He's going to need you and his dad in the days to come." She'd paused to gather her breath and strength. "Don't let him forget that he needs his dad. In their hurt, they'll pull away from each other, but his dad needs Chace just as much as Chace needs his dad."

The memory faded. We stood silent, one on either side of our dragon. The surf lapped at the rocks, and the ropes tying our boat to the dock creaked. How could I encourage Chace to come home? A seagull called overhead, and Steria stirred, looking up at it. This close, I could feel her flash of yearning to soar with the bird.

"Harley, you can go now," Chace said. "The others are waiting for you."

"No, Chace, the others are waiting for *us*. Steria, help me, here. He can't leave his dad to stay with you. Besides, if he stays, that means we'll have more trips back and forth, and Professor Raleigh would be more likely to find you."

Steria bent her neck and dipped her head, much like I'd seen horses do. *That is your job, Harley.* Her voice sounded quiet in my mind. *He will not listen to me. I have tried.*

So much for the easy route. I sighed.

"Chace, I know it's hard, but look at Steria. Really look at her. Feel what she's feeling."

I paused and took my own advice. Peace filled me. It seemed to wrap its way around us. Then a breeze touched my face. It didn't break the peace, but instead brought a longing—a longing to chase it, to be free, to roam far and wide. As the wind died down, that longing was replaced with contentment.

Steria stood and stretched, looking like an overgrown cat with wings. She turned and placed her forehead against Chace's and gently pressed in. Chace wrapped his arms around her neck. They stood that way for the longest time. I didn't want to leave without Chace, but I didn't want to intrude, either. Finally, she stepped away and looked at both of us.

Thank you for all you have done. You both believed when others didn't. You kept me safe. Now, go, live with your loved ones. I will be fine, but there are others who need you.

She turned, crouched, and lifted into the air. We stood alone and watched as she joined some sea birds cavorting overhead, then peeled away and followed some pelicans fishing further out along the waves. With a graceful swoop, she dragged her hind feet through the water and came away with what I assumed must be a fish. She took her prize to a rocky outcropping jutting up out of the water and set to it with obvious delight. We could just make out her silhouette.

Chace stirred, bringing me back to myself.

"Well, Harley." His voice cracked, and he swallowed. "Let's go home. Dad will be worried about me."

CHAPTER 23: A SOLEMN WARNING

THE RIDE HOME was quiet, each of us lost in our own little world. We arrived back at Myrtle Beach just as the sun set. The marina was vacant except for Mom—Mr. Behr had called her to meet us. She didn't look very happy, but she greeted each of us kids with a hug.

"Thank you for bringing them back home safely," she told him.

"Mrs. Meagher, they never really were in danger."

I thought of the professor shooting at me and decided it was best Mom didn't know that.

"Nevertheless, I thank you." She pulled Karis and me closer to her.

"Aw, Mom," I said.

She just shook her head to silence me. I complied.

"Let's go home," she said. "Chace, you're spending the night with us; you're dad's out on a fishing run still. Will and Cherise, I'm to drop you off at your homes."

"Thank you, Mrs. Meagher," Mr. Behr said. "I'll head on home, too. Let me know if you need anything."

He waved and walked to the only other car in the parking lot.

Will slid the boat key into his pocket and did a final check to make sure all the lines were tied off, then joined us. Mom turned, one arm still around Karis and the other around me, and headed to the car.

* * *

The next morning, I was awakened by a knock on my bedroom door.

"Harley," Mom called. "Harley, you and Chace have company."

I rubbed the sleep from my eyes. Who would visit us? How would anyone even know Chace was here?

After a quick change of clothes, we trundled downstairs after Mom into the guest parlor. Standing staring out the window was the man who had plagued my nightmares, his hands stuck casually in his pockets. At a creak from the floorboards, he turned.

"Thank you, Mrs. Meagher."

Mom nodded and walked out of the room. Feelings of betrayal and abandonment washed over me as I watched her shut the door behind her.

"Have a seat, boys," the professor said.

He ran a hand through his hair. His tie was loosened, his suit jacket askew, and he looked like he hadn't slept all night. A part of me felt sorry for him, but the other part still felt the impact of the sticky web he had shot at me. I didn't want to sit down, but I knew he wouldn't steal us away from Mom, and there was *no* way he was learning where we had taken Steria. So I sat. Chace followed suit, but I noticed that he seated himself on the very edge of the sofa. The professor paced.

"Do you boys have any clue the trouble you've caused me?"

"We've caused *you*?" Chace exclaimed. I nudged him, but it didn't stop him. "You came on my property without permission; you insulted my dad and me; you chased us across town and *shot* at Harley! I'd say *you* caused us trouble."

Professor Raleigh paused in his tracks and slumped into a chair with a heavy exhalation.

"You're right, Chace. I've spent the night on the phone with my supervisor chewing me out. I've made a mess of everything. Normally, I'm not supposed to let civilians even know who I am or what I do." He paused and ran a hand through his hair again.

I wasn't ready to forgive him or even feel sorry for him, but I could at least listen.

"So?" Chace asked, his chin thrust out stubbornly. "Why are you here?"

Professor Raleigh sat back and looked us straight in the eyes. "Boys, I'm going to go against everything my higher-ups have told me to do. They haven't been here, haven't met you. I have to do what I think is best."

We waited, and I saw Chace roll his eyes. The professor didn't seem to notice, or if he did, he didn't say anything about it. Despite saying he'd made a decision, he still seemed conflicted. Finally, he huffed out a breath and continued.

"As I told Harley, the dragon came through a continuum warp. For some reason, Myrtle Beach is one of those keystones that attracts the fantasy realm. The space between the two worlds grows thin, and fantasy creatures are escaping. My job is to capture those animals and return them to a special farm where they are prevented from harming our world and safe from prying eyes. However, wherever you took the dragon is far enough out of range of my sensors that I believe it will be safe."

"*She'll* be safe," Chace corrected.

Professor Raleigh raised an eyebrow, but nodded. "She'll be safe. So, I'm going to let her stay wherever she is. I'm not going to ask where. I know you won't tell me anyway." He stood and took out his wallet. From it he produced a pair of business cards, distributing one to each of us. "If anything happens, and she's no longer able to stay where you took her, give me a call. I'll take her to our preserve. Until then, I hope not to hear from you."

He walked out the front door. I sat staring at the card in my hand. Chace laughed. I looked up to see an elated grin covering his face.

"Harley, do you realize what this means? We can visit Steria whenever we want!"

I shook my head. "I don't think so, Chace. I don't trust him. Maybe later, after some time has passed we can go, but… for now, I'm afraid he's just waiting for us to lead him to her."

Chace's face fell. "You think so?"

I nodded ruefully. "Sorry to disappoint you."

"You're probably right," Chace said, but he was obviously crushed.

"At least she should be safe there," I offered weakly.

"Yeah."

We sat in silence for a while, warmed by the rays of sun that streamed in through the windows. On the wall, an old cuckoo clock ticked away, the only sound in the room. At last, I stretched and looked over at my friend.

"Want to go swimming?" I asked.

"Sure." His smile showed the hurt underneath, but at least it was genuine. "Let's ask Karis if she wants to take us all up to your place. Maybe your dad will be back by now as well."

He nodded, and we left the silent room behind and ran upstairs to get my sister.

AN UNEXPECTED ESCAPADE:

CHAPTER 1

THE TINKLING OF the stream greeted Kajri's ears, as it always did when she crested the hill. She descended into the little valley and lowered her head to drink, satisfying her thirst in the crystalline water. Dust motes danced in the streams of sunlight filtering through the trees. Her muzzle still damp, she moved to the nearest ray and smiled as her single pearlescent horn pierced the light. Lifting her hooves with a gentle movement, she pranced about the small clearing, soaking in the warmth of the sun and reveling in the joy that could only belong to those who made the wood their home.

Stopping suddenly, Kajri pricked her ears straight up, her attention wholly focused on the sound. Was it a voice? It was as if another language flowed from female lips. With slow movements, Kajri tilted her head and flicked her ears to gather the words closer, but the language still eluded her. Just as abruptly as the first sound had arisen, another overlaid it. Kajri pinioned her ears against her skull to shut out the shrill squeal. Her body went taut, muscles gathering to flee. Turning, she tried to run, only to find her hooves no longer touched the ground. Her forelock fluttered into her eyes, and she shook her head, trying to move it aside.

Just as inexplicably as they'd left it, her hooves gained purchase on the forest floor, and Kajri ran, dodging trees and roots in a desperate panic.   At last, the screeching finally faded into the distance. Once she was confident it wouldn't return, Kajri slowed to a trot and then to a walk, her sides heaving. She blinked and came to a standstill as cold drops began to pelt her skin. Her skin shivered and water dripped into her eyes. She looked around her. What had happened? Her own familiar forest had disappeared, and in its place lay a vista of rolling hills with evergreen trees. Where was she?

If you enjoyed *An Unexpected Adventure*, you may be interested in other books by the same author. If you wish to learn about special promotions and the release of new books by Kandi J Wyatt, you can sign up for her newsletter and find all the places to connect with her at kandijwyatt.com.

More from Kandi J Wyatt
Middle Grade Fantasy
Journey from Skioria

Dragon Courage Series
Dragon's Future
Dragon's Heir
Dragon's Revenge
Dragon's Cure
Dragon's Posterity
Dragon's Heritage

Myth Coast Adventures
An Unexpected Adventure
An Unexpected Escapade (spring, 2019)
An Unintended Adventure (fall, 2019)

Biblical Retellings
The One Who Sees Me (historical fiction)
To Save a Race (steampunk)

Made in the USA
San Bernardino, CA
26 July 2020